The elderly pati
Jakob.

'Mebbe you two should ... ... New Year
t'gether, then.'

Kirsten remembered what usually happened when
the clock struck twelve. Friends, even complete
strangers, would hug and kiss. Without thinking,
she scanned his broad shoulders, his rugged face,
his firm lips, imagining.

A shiver of awareness shot through her as his
gaze focused on her mouth. An intent, hungry
spark lit his eyes, making it obvious that his
thoughts were traveling along the same path.

Dear Reader

I'm delighted to introduce you to Bethany, Kirsten and Naomi in the *Sisters at Heart* trilogy. I've always enjoyed reading books with a common thread and wanted to create one of my own. Someday.

When a close friend moved to another community, I knew that 'someday' had arrived. While bemoaning the lost opportunities for spur-of-the-moment walks and the lack of a readily available sypathetic ear, I couldn't help but reminisce about my other close friends. I have a special place in my heart for those who accepted me into their circle when I, as a teenager, advanced from small country schools to one with nearly a thousand students. We laughed together and cried together, shared our dreams and aspirations, and weathered the storms on our way to adulthood.

Consequently, when I met Beth for the first time, I understood how important her friends were to her and saw how their early camaraderie shaped their lives, making them as emotionally close as sisters. They shared many experiences and interests, and from that this series came into being.

I invite you to meet three women whose friendship has withstood the test of time. I hope that you, too, have several friends who are your 'sisters at heart'.

Happy Reading!

Jessica Matthews

A HEART
OF GOLD

BY
JESSICA MATTHEWS

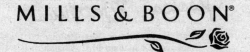

MILLS & BOON®

To Judy, the best sister a girl could have.

*First published in Great Britain 1997
Harlequin Mills & Boon Limited,
Eton House, 18-24 Paradise Road, Richmond, Surrey TW9 1SR*

© Jessica Matthews 1997

ISBN 0 263 80432 1

*Set in Times 10 on 11½ pt. by
Rowland Phototypesetting Limited
Bury St Edmunds, Suffolk*

03-9710-46528-D

*Oxford Dictionary of Nursery Rhymes, edited by Iona and Peter Opie.
First published 1951. Extracts used by permission of
Oxford University Press.*

Printed and bound in Great Britain
by Mackays of Chatham PLC, Chatham

CHAPTER ONE

OLD MOTHER HUBBARD, went to the cupboard . . .

The nursery rhyme popped into Dr Kirsten Holloway's mind as she escorted her distinguished visitor around her clinic, the Family Health Center. How inconvenient that four-year-old Amanda Jenkins's repertoire of pre-school verses should stick in her thoughts now.

At another time Kirsten would have indulged herself with a stroll down memory lane, recalling the same childhood verses that she, too, had memorized and repeated just as faithfully and accurately to any listening adult ear. At this moment, however, she couldn't afford the distraction. Dr Jakob Marshall, with his athletic frame as stiff as the collar of his white dress shirt and his attitude as chilly as the late December afternoon, wouldn't appreciate a Mother Goose commentary.

Determined to send the pre-school poems back into the dim recesses of her brain, Kirsten rubbed her forehead before she pointed to a door only a few steps down the hallway. 'If you'll follow me I'll show you where we store our medication.'

Dutifully he stepped aside.

During the few seconds it took to reach their destination her gaze wandered over the man's short light brown hair, wishing that her own possessed a small portion of his natural wave. Finding only a few threads of gray, her attention landed on his craggy features. She noted his high forehead, the inch-long scar over his left

5

eyebrow, his pronounced cheek-bones, straight nose and firm chin.

Overall, his aristocratic features and bearing commanded respect, whereas her own pixie-like face with its retroussé nose generated the opposite. People, including her medical school instructors and fellow students, tended to take her at face value until they recognized the intelligence lurking underneath a winsome exterior.

Wondering what it would take to draw him into conversation, Kirsten offered a huge smile and turned the doorknob. His silence made her feel like a teenager showing off her first car—a used Ford—to a friend who owned a BMW.

'We try to stock a wide variety of drugs, mostly run-of-the-mill items. None of the controlled substances, though.'

. . . to fetch her poor dog a bone.

She took a deep breath, struggling to keep her mind on her task. 'They're mostly samples, donated by the various drug company reps. We get some from local physicians, too.' Taking time to peer inside, Kirsten noticed its near-empty condition.

And when she got there, the cupboard was bare . . .

She swallowed hard. Only a few boxes of nasal decongestant, muscle relaxant, acetaminophen and an antibiotic graced the shelves—certainly nothing to brag about. No doubt his own office stock could compete with a full-service pharmacy. Squaring her shoulders, she mentally dared him to make a comment.

None came.

She brushed at the wispy bangs on her forehead and stared at the taciturn cardiologist, conscious of his broad shoulders so near to her own. At five feet seven she had never described herself as short, but next to him—even though he stood a mere five or six inches taller—she felt small. Not small in a negative sense, but small in a petite, feminine way.

Considering that he hadn't shown even a glimmer of personal interest, she couldn't understand her reaction.

'Normally we have a lot more on hand,' she said, not quite sure why she sounded defensive, 'but the colder temperatures have brought us a record number of patients. The majority of them can't pay for a doctor's visit, much less any medication.'

'So you provide it,' he stated.

'Yes.' The deep timbre of his voice caught her off guard, and for an instant she couldn't choke out another word. His blue-gray gaze lingered on hers as it had since their introduction. It wasn't surprising—new acquaintances usually focused on her unique trait of one blue and one green eye. Her auburn hair—striking in its own right, according to her friends—made the unusual combination all the more obvious.

Strangers' scrutiny had never bothered her before, but somehow Jakob Marshall's did. She clasped her hands together.

'And what happens if you don't have it to give? Like now?' He pointed to the closet.

And so her poor dog had none.

Kirsten rubbed the back of her neck, forcefully derailing her thoughts off the childish track. 'We give our patients a voucher to take to a nearby pharmacy. The owner provides medication at generous discounts.'

She wished the closet had been at least half-full to prove that the individuals in this poor neighborhood received high-quality medicine in spite of their inability to pay. Then again perhaps the empty shelves spoke more eloquently than she ever could.

At the same time she wondered if he'd noticed that the boxes weren't in their designated places. The antibiotics sat on the shelf labelled for diuretics, and the muscle relaxants resided in the location for cardiac drugs. Meeting his piercing scrutiny, she doubted—with a measure of disappointment since she intended to impress—if anything escaped his notice.

'Excuse me, Dr Holloway,' Amy Gartin, the center's nurse, interrupted. 'Miss Grant is ready. Upper respiratory symptoms.' The twenty-seven-year-old's dark eyes gleamed with curiosity over their visitor.

Kirsten turned to Jakob. 'This won't take long. If you'd like to wait in my office. . .'

'I'd rather observe, if you don't mind,' he said. 'It's been years since my family practice days.'

His baritone sent a strange shiver down her spine.

Humpty Dumpty sat on a wall, Humpty Dumpty had a great fall . . .

She swallowed. 'This particular patient is very—shall we say—vocal with her opinions.'

Jakob's eyes sparkled and the corners of his well-formed mouth twitched. 'Afraid she'll hurt my feelings, Dr Holloway? Damage my self-esteem, perhaps?'

Kirsten doubted whether anyone or anything could. He appeared too self-assured to let anyone's comments affect him. 'She doesn't like male doctors.'

'A charming woman, I'm sure.'

Certain she couldn't dissuade him, she said, 'Suit yourself.'

Jakob thrust out his arm in an 'after you' gesture and followed her.

Hilda Grant, her thin eighty-year-old frame bent from the effects of osteoporosis common to the elderly, sat on the table with her feet dangling several inches above the floor. With painstaking slowness, her gnarled fingers rolled the sleeve cuffs of her worn but clean pink sweat-shirt above her wrists.

'What seems to be the trouble today, Hilda?' Kirsten asked, noticing the woman's pallor and deciding that she looked as tired and gray as her short, limp hair.

'Who's he?' Hilda replied instead, scrutinizing Kirsten's visitor through narrowed and faded green eyes.

Before Kirsten could introduce him Jakob stepped forward. 'I'm Dr Marshall.'

Although clearly suspicious, Hilda placed one wrinkled hand in his proffered one. With the other she picked at the sleeve of his dark blue suit coat. 'I worked fer a dry-cleaners in my time. Recognize quality when I see it.'

'Thank you,' he said.

'You slummin' today? I s'pose you're like all the other rich people. Ya get ta feelin' guilty over the holidays so ya pop in on us poor folk, drop a few bucks, then go your merry way with a clear conscience.'

Although Kirsten suspected that he had come for the very reason Hilda had described, she found the old woman's candor embarrassing. She broke in to change the subject. 'So you're not feeling well.'

'Course I'm not,' Hilda snapped. 'I wouldn' a come otherwise.' She stared up at Jakob. 'Well? Is that why you're here? Got a case of the guilts?'

'No,' he replied.

'Hah.'

Kirsten scanned Amy's notes while listening to the exchange. If he didn't suffer from a guilty conscience then he had to be interested in a tax break. Why else would a man of his caliber and obvious social standing drop into their humble establishment?

Regardless of his motives, she intended to show him that this center was worthy of his financial support.

Little Tommy Tucker sings for his supper . . . Oh, dear, she thought, stifling a sigh. Here we go again.

'I'm not takin' my clothes off in front of *him*.' Hilda folded her thin arms over her chest.

'You won't need to,' Kirsten said.

'Good. Like I told the nurse, I got a runny nose. Head hurts. My face, too. Junk drains down my throat an' makes me cough.'

Kirsten reached for a tongue depressor. 'Open wide.' After checking Hilda's throat and ears, she pressed on her cheek-bones. 'Does that hurt?'

'Yeah.'

Kirsten unwrapped the stethoscope around her neck and warmed the diaphragm between her palms. Conscious of Hilda's modesty, she listened to her patient's lung and heart sounds without raising the shirt above her patient's midriff.

'Are there lady undertakers?' Hilda asked.

'I don't know,' Kirsten answered, pausing to wonder what had prompted the question.

'If'n I die I don't want no man to see me neked. It jus' ain't right for men to handle dead women. No tellin' what they'd do. Especially with me never been married.'

At a loss for words, Kirsten glanced at Jakob. The wry twist to his mouth suggested that he found the comment humorous but, instead of joining in the conversation, he raised one eyebrow in an I'm-anxious-to-hear-your-answer gesture.

She cleared her throat. 'A funeral director will be happy to discuss their procedures with you so my advice is to call them. Now, take a deep breath, please.'

A few minutes later Kirsten replaced the stethoscope

around her neck. 'Everything looks fine except your sinuses, but an antibiotic will soon clear the infection.'

Hurrying out of the room, she grabbed several of the remaining cartons in her drug stock and rushed back. She didn't want to leave Hilda alone with him too long for fear of what else she might say in her usual forthright manner.

She thrust a packet into Hilda's hand. 'Take one of these pills twice a day until you run out. Then stop by again and Amy will give you more.' Handing her another box, she said, 'This is your decongestant. Take these twice a day as well.'

Hilda stared at the labels. 'You sure this'll work, Dr Holloway?' she asked in her hoarse voice, distrust obvious on her aged features. 'I don' trust stuff with fancy names. Could be poison.'

Kirsten didn't pronounce the generic chemicals, knowing from past experience that her patient wouldn't leave until she, too, could say the words without stumbling over every syllable. Today, due to Jakob Marshall's presence, she didn't have time for a phonics lesson.

She took a deep breath. 'Believe me, it's not poison. You should feel better in a week or so.'

'Stores say things are new and improved, then call 'em somethin' else,' Hilda continued, 'but it's usually the same old whatever only in a diff'rent package.' She leaned closer. 'That way they can charge them higher prices and get away with it.'

Kirsten smiled. Each time she'd given Hilda anything other than penicillin the senior citizen had resorted to her familiar lament. 'Just remember to follow my instructions and you'll be better before long.'

Hilda bobbed her head in understanding.

'And use a pain-reliever if necessary.'

'Don't have none. Ran out this mornin'.'

Having anticipated that possibility, Kirsten placed one last package into Hilda's hands. 'Now you do.'

'By the way, those high-falutin vitamins you give me last time I was in are almost gone.'

'The calcium and Vitamin D?'

Hilda nodded.

. . . The cupboard was bare . . .

'I don't have any right now, but come back in a day or two.' Kirsten made a mental note to add Hilda's supplements to the long list of supplies she needed to purchase. Thanks to the check in today's mail, she had the money to do so. Unfortunately, according to the accompanying letter, their nameless benefactor's generosity was about to come to an end.

'Are you having any back pain?' Kirsten asked.

Hilda shook her gray head.

'Are the "Meals on Wheels" people still coming?' Kirsten had ruled out estrogen therapy for a variety of reasons so a proper diet was crucial. Until the elderly woman had come to the clinic she'd lived a hand-to-mouth existence, thrilled to eat whatever she could find—regardless of its nutritional value.

'Like clockwork.' Hilda leaned forward, her grin revealing yellowed teeth. 'Sure am glad you fixed it to have the food delivered. Beats scroungin' or goin' without. Course I don't care for the spinach they send ever' now 'n then, but what the heck.' She shrugged.

Kirsten smiled. Satisfied that she'd done all she could, she filled Hilda's voluminous purse with the samples before she reached out to help her off the exam table. Clutching Hilda's upper arm, she felt the woman's bones through the long sleeves.

To her surprise, Jakob moved to Hilda's side and

took the old woman's hand in his, offering his strength without a word.

'Steady now.' Kirsten watched Hilda find her footing, noticing the incongruous picture they made—Hilda's red socks and black sandals with a broken strap, Dr Marshall's polished Italian loafers and her scuffed Reeboks.

Once she was certain that the woman could solo, Kirsten released her hold. 'Be careful outside. The weather forecast is rain, changing to snow.'

Hilda nodded. 'I'm on my way home. Don' plan to get out.' She peered up at Kirsten. 'You partyin' tonight?'

Kirsten chuckled. 'Afraid not.' In years past she'd enjoyed quiet holidays with her close friends, Beth Trahern and Naomi Stewart. But Beth had married Tristan Lockwood three years ago and lived a hundred miles away. Naomi had the dubious honor of drawing the graveyard shift at Lakeside Memorial.

Even so, if she'd wanted to usher in the New Year with the proverbial bang she couldn't. She had to come up with a strategy to save the clinic. . .and her job.

Hilda turned to face Jakob. 'What about you?'

He blinked. 'I don't plan to go out either.'

'You married?'

He shook his head.

'Hmm. Neither is she.' Hilda's eyes darted back and forth between Kirsten and Jakob. 'Mebbe you two should welcome the New Year t'gether, then.'

Kirsten remembered what usually happened when the clock struck twelve. Friends, even complete strangers, would hug and kiss, wishing each other a happy New Year. Without thinking, she scanned his broad shoulders, his rugged face, his firm lips, imagining such an event with him at her side.

A shiver of awareness shot through her as his gaze focused on her mouth. An intent, hungry spark lit his eyes, making it obvious that his thoughts were traveling along the same path that hers were.

Immediately recognizing the folly of her daydreams, Kirsten reined in her wayward imagination. 'I couldn't—'

'Afraid not—' he said at the same moment.

Hilda shrugged. 'Might help ya' both loosen up. Get rid of them bags under yer eyes and take the starch outa his unmentionables.'

Kirsten held her breath, wondering how Jakob would receive Hilda's blunt characterization. Although Jakob's stern, no-nonsense demeanor suggested that he took life far too seriously, she wished that the woman had kept her opinion to herself.

'I'll bear your advice in mind,' Jakob said, his tone dry but without malice.

Kirsten let out her breath.

Hilda shuffled to the door. 'Course, I never could understand people celebratin'. Jus' another year, anyways. Prob'ly worse than the last one,' she mumbled, before making her exit.

Kirsten sincerely hoped that the woman's words weren't prophetic. She couldn't imagine the upcoming year being worse than the one about to enter the annals of history.

The new year simply had to be better.

Once they were alone Kirsten faced her visitor. With an apologetic shrug, she slid her hands into her lab coat's pockets. 'I warned you.'

The lines around his mouth softened. 'Yes, you did. That's one advantage of growing old—you can say and do whatever's on your mind.'

His reserve make her wonder what would make him smile. Had he, in his quest for success, forgotten how?

He interrupted her thoughts. 'Are all of your patients indigent?'

'No,' she answered, listening for a lofty, condescending tone and hearing none. 'We cater to those who fall through the cracks in the system; the so-called "working poor". Many of our clients have jobs but, by virtue of a few dollars, are disqualified from government assistance. At the same time, they don't earn enough to afford private health insurance.'

Kirsten followed his gaze around the room. She saw her domain through his eyes, noticing the well-worn upholstery on the exam table, the chair with the wobbly leg and the counter-tops with the speckled design worn off in places. The only things gleaming in the room were the actual medical instruments—a gift from a sponsor three years earlier. In spite of their relative newness, they were beginning to show the dull signs of wear.

'We provide durable medical equipment, too— crutches, walkers, wheelchairs, and so on—through a loan program.'

Jakob's face remained impassive and Kirsten felt compelled to continue. 'We also accept disposable diapers and baby formula.' She grimaced. 'The demand often exceeds the supply.'

'And do you share these items with your middle-income patients?'

Kirsten's hackles rose at his innuendo and her voice turned cool. 'We dispense everything we have based on need and availability, not according to a bank balance. Everyone who walks through the front door gets treated the same.'

He quirked one eyebrow. 'No one takes advantage of your generosity?'

'A few, but not enough to warrant a change in policy.'

'I see.' His noncommittal tone made it difficult for Kirsten to decide if he agreed with her convictions or had simply acknowledged the information.

'How long have you worked here?' he asked.

'Since I finished my family practice residency six months ago.' If he wanted to know that she was twenty-nine then he could figure it out for himself. 'I met Diana Morrison during my internship and, since we had similar philosophies, she invited me to join her.'

'Now you're on your own.'

He'd obviously heard of Diana's untimely death in a car accident. 'Yes. Did you know her?'

'We'd met. A long time ago.'

Wondering if Diana's demise had piqued his curiosity, she fished for an answer to the question uppermost in her mind—why had he come? 'She would have been delighted to know you have a special interest in our cause.'

He crossed his arms and leaned against the counter. With his brow wrinkled in thought, he appeared as if he had to decide what to say and then search for the right words. 'Yes, well, I find myself in a somewhat strange position. I need to return a favor. Right a wrong, so to speak.'

His cryptic comment puzzled her. 'Oh?'

'What do you need the most?' he asked, apparently disregarding her bid for more details. 'Supplies or money?'

Kirsten blinked. Either gift would be a help, especially one of cold, hard cash now that their major source was drying up like a pond during a drought. Yet the ache between her shoulders reminded her of something else the clinic needed—another doctor. She'd worked seven days a week for so long that she doubted whether her neighbors recognized her any more.

'Rich people. . .get ta feelin' guilty. . .drop a few bucks. . .go your merry way with a clear conscience.'

Kirsten heard Hilda's succinct comments in her mind as clearly as if she'd just spoken them. Although Kirsten accepted each donation with joy she admitted the truth. Their few sponsors were willing to dig in their pockets rather than give something more precious—their time and talent.

'Either would be appreciated,' she said. Then, whether it was due to Hilda's candor rubbing off, her own tiredness, or the fact that she wanted to make this particular affluent member of the medical community pay for the stinginess of one so long ago, she added, 'But we have a critical need for something else.'

His expression became guarded. 'What's that?'

She bolstered her courage. 'Staffing—at least on a part-time basis. I'm desperate for another doctor, or at least a physician's assistant, who's willing to work for next to nothing. Do you know of anyone?'

A look of pain crossed his face, although she couldn't understand why. She hadn't asked for a cardiologist or implied that *he* should fill in the gap, even though she had a fair number of patients who were heart attacks waiting to happen.

She schooled her features into a polite mask but inwardly she smiled. More people—especially those like Dr Marshall—needed to know that a check didn't always provide the answer.

'Can't you hire someone?' he asked.

'I've tried. As you know, graduating physicians

usually have huge debts. They've scraped by for so long that they're ready to reap financial benefits, not struggle along on the small salary I can offer. Considering what assistants can earn, even they aren't interested.'

Jakob pursed his mouth, as if pondering her request. 'I see.' He straightened to his full height. 'Thanks for your time. I'll be in touch.'

Kirsten could tell a brush-off when she heard one. Disappointment rose inside her. She stifled its note hovering in her throat and forced a cool reply between her clenched teeth. 'Of course. Can you find your way out?'

'Yes. Thanks again.'

She nodded, too disheartened to speak.

While Jakob headed down the hallway, past the receptionist and out the front entrance, Kirsten stomped to her tiny office. She stripped her lab coat off and tossed it over the pile of journals, stacked haphazardly on a footstool. With movements born out of frustration, she tugged on the hem of her red Santa sweatshirt until the bottom edge rested on her black denim-clad hips.

Her second-hand desk chair creaked as she plunked herself onto the thick cushion she'd bought at a department store. Picking up a ballpoint pen, she doodled dollar signs on a scratch pad while she wished for a bag of her favorite snack food—extra-salty pretzels.

Her doodles changed into faces—funny faces wearing the same shocked expression Dr Marshall had worn. It was clear that he'd been appalled by the idea of physically helping the less fortunate.

Just like the man who, twenty years earlier, had refused to treat her little sister.

Out of habit, her attention shifted to the ragged-looking clown doll displayed on top of the file cabinet across the room. Over two decades later the rainbow colors of the toy's polka-dot garments had faded, but the memory of its owner had not. And never would.

Her opinion of Marshall sank at the same time as she berated herself. She should have chosen one of his two options, namely money. At least she'd have *something* to show for the time she'd spent with him.

Amy strode into the room and plopped down in a chair matching Kirsten's. 'How did it go? I've sent the last patient home so don't spare any details.'

Kirsten's squiggles grew fainter in spite of the pressure she applied. She threw the pen into the trash can, before meeting the brunette nurse's gaze.

'I screwed up. Royally.'

Amy's eyes widened. 'What did you do?'

Kirsten leaned back. 'He asked what we needed—supplies or money. I said I was desperate for a doctor.'

'At least you were honest.'

'Yeah, and evidently it was more than he could stomach because he left shortly afterwards.' She frowned. 'I should have smiled and told him we'd accept whatever he wanted to give. Now we have nothing.'

'Maybe he just has to think things over.'

'I doubt it.' Kirsten ran her fingers through her bangs. 'Let's face it. Diana had a knack for squeezing whatever she needed out of a turnip. I don't.'

'You're forgetting that she learned a lot from her father while he operated the clinic. In time, you'll learn the ins and outs, too.'

'Time is a luxury we don't have.' At Amy's incredulous expression, Kirsten wordlessly handed her a page of cream-colored stationery, bearing the logo of a local bank.

Amy glanced at the money order stapled to the paper.

'What's the fuss? A ten-thousand dollar check isn't too shabby.'

'No, but it won't last long, especially if we have several patients needing the more sophisticated diagnostic procedures like CT scans or magnetic resonance imaging.'

'I see what you mean.' While the nurse scanned the page the windows rattled from a sudden gust of wind. At long last Amy quoted one sentence aloud, her former excitement giving way to anger. ' "He regrets having to end his generosity at this time, and apologizes for any inconvenience this may cause." '

Amy stared at Kirsten. 'What will we do when it's gone?'

Kirsten pretended a confidence she didn't feel. 'We'll manage. There are others who'd be happy to help us, I'm sure.' If only she could find them. Soon.

Amy's troubled expression cleared. 'That's what I like about you, Dr Holloway,' she remarked, using a formality she reserved for when patients were present. 'You never lose hope.'

Kirsten smiled. Hope was the only thing she had in abundance.

'Hey, you two.' Irene Garcia, the forty-two-year-old receptionist—and Spanish translator whenever the need arose—spoke from the doorway. 'In case you haven't noticed, it's time to go home.'

'Ready to celebrate?' Kirsten teased.

'Of course. Miguel is smoking a turkey. You're both welcome to join us.'

'I'd like to, but I have a date,' Amy said.

'You don't sound thrilled,' Irene noted.

Amy wrinkled her nose. 'A blind date. One that my *mother* arranged, no less.'

Irene addressed Kirsten. 'How about you? We'd love for you to come.'

Kirsten eyed the various stacks in front of her. 'We'll see. I'd like to start the new year off with a semi-clean desk.'

'Good heavens!' Amy was aghast. 'You'll be here for hours.'

'I know, but I can't put it off any longer.' Kirsten softened her next sentence with a grin. 'Not to be rude, but the sooner you both leave the sooner I'll get started.'

The nurse jumped to her feet and struck an affronted pose. 'Well, I can tell where we're not wanted. Just for that, we won't come back until next year.'

Irene giggled. 'You bet.'

Kirsten fixed her smile into place until she heard their voices fade and the back door click. Resting in her chair, she rubbed her forehead and closed her eyes. Discarding the optimistic façade she'd hidden behind for Amy's sake, she opened the floodgates of despair.

She'd been here for six months, and for the last four she'd fought an uphill battle for survival. The clinic couldn't fold—she wouldn't let it. The people in this neighborhood had counted on Diana Morrison when they couldn't receive help anywhere else. Now those same people counted on her.

She could never live with herself if she let them down.

Nor could she live with herself if her failure caused another child like her sister to die because he or she had fallen through the cracks in the system.

The new year *would* be better, she vowed again. Surely the worst was over and the storm had passed. And if she needed to grovel before men like Jakob Marshall she would.

For some reason, the mere mention of his name

conjured up his image so vividly that his presence, including his cologne, seemed to manifest itself in the room.

Disregarding her fanciful imagination, she delved into the lab reports that needed her review. For the next few hours the easy-listening radio station provided background music as she scratched notes with a cheap ballpoint pen and rustled through what seemed like reams of paper.

Occasionally a muted roar of automobile engines and the whistle of wind against the windows jarred the tranquility. By the time the afternoon sun faded into dusk, she'd moved all the correspondence from her 'In' basket to the one designated 'Out'.

Pleased with her progress, Kirsten clicked off the radio, shrugged into her parka and made her way to the back exit. Each flip of a fluorescent light switch increased the gloom until only the Exit sign lit the darkness.

Bracing herself against the cold, she stepped outside—and plowed into a man in a dark gray trench coat with the collar turned up against the wind. A strangled scream burst from her throat before she recognized her previous visitor.

'Dr Marshall! Did you forget something?' Searching her office in her mind's eye for a hat or pair of gloves, she drew a blank.

'No.'

Her teeth chattered. 'Then what are you doing here?'

'Waiting for you.' His breath made white vapor clouds in the frigid air.

From the looks of his reddened cheeks, he'd been waiting for some time. 'Oh?'

'You mentioned that you needed more help. A

doctor—or a physician's assistant, to be exact.' His gaze, more gray than blue this time, didn't waver.

'Yes.' She drew out the word, puzzled by the direction he seemed to be heading.

Cupping his hands over his mouth and nose, Jakob took a deep breath before he thrust them inside his pockets. His mouth moved slowly, as if his facial muscles were too numb to work properly.

'Will you settle for me?'

CHAPTER TWO

STANDING close enough to feel Jakob's body heat, Kirsten watched her frosty breath merge into his. Mesmerized by the sight, it took a gust of cold wind across her face to bring her to her senses.

'I think we should discuss this inside.' Kirsten dug in her pockets for the key, then unlocked the outer door. She snapped on the lights and led Jakob to her office, before taking his coat and hanging it on a hook next to hers.

Meanwhile, her mind reeled from his unexpected offer. If he'd given money or supplies, or volunteered to act as a consultant, she'd have taken his comment in stride. But becoming a member of the staff? It was too outlandish to believe.

Still cold, she sat on the edge of her desk and rubbed her hands together. While he took the side chair she collected her scattered thoughts. 'Let me get this straight. You're proposing to work here?'

He crossed his long legs and nodded.

'Part time.'

'Tuesdays and Thursdays would work out best,' he replied without hesitation.

'I appreciate the thought, but I don't understand why you're willing to sign on with us when the position is beneath your skills.'

'Do the reasons matter?' he parried.

'I suppose not,' Kirsten admitted. 'Although I find it a little hard to believe. If you were—' She cut herself off.

'Right out of residency? An idealistic young doctor?'

His words stung. Her voice turned cool. 'A family practitioner.'

'I started in family practice before I switched to internal medicine. Does that count?'

'What about your patients? If the medical grapevine can be believed, you carry a tremendous load—especially with all of the referrals you receive.'

'My clients won't suffer.'

'If you're not available. . .' She let her question go unasked.

'Someone else in my group will be.' He changed position. 'Perhaps I should explain the situation more clearly.'

'Please do.' Finally some answers, she thought.

'The Marshall Clinic is expanding and, in order to do that, we've started an extensive remodeling project. Rather than try to conduct business while the work is being done, we're closing the office two days a week and extending our hours on the other three. Emergencies are, of course, seen at the hospital.'

'But why work here? You said yourself that it's been a long time since you were involved in a general practice. Why should I hire you?'

'Because you're desperate and don't have a choice. In spite of my so-called limitations, I'm better than nothing. Wouldn't you agree?'

Kirsten's face warmed at his blunt but factual remarks.

'If I run into a case I can't handle I'll bow to your experience.'

She couldn't tell if he meant to be reassuring or facetious. And, to be honest, the potential for a confrontation hadn't escaped her. She didn't want the health center to become a battleground because he, having specialized training and more years of experience, wouldn't defer to a younger physician.

She straightened. 'Just *certain* cases?'

His eyes glimmered, as if he'd found her reaction humorous. 'Being a cardiologist, I haven't totally forgotten or lost my internal medicine skills. I was referring to obstetrics and pediatrics.'

She relaxed.

'I would also expect the same courtesy.'

'Of course. However, spending half of your profitable working hours here doesn't make sense. If you'd suggested a day here or there, or agreed to be a consultant for select cases. . .' She let her voice die.

'As I mentioned earlier, I'm repaying an old debt. I know it sounds mysterious, but it isn't. I'd rather keep the boring details to myself.'

She brushed at her bangs, mulling over the situation. If Jakob Marshall had been a family physician she'd sign him on in a heartbeat. Yet if he, being a highly trained and experienced cardiologist, wasn't worrying over his private patients why should she? He knew his own business—knew how long he could maintain his practice under such limited conditions.

And if Dr Marshall chose to discharge his obligations by working at a clinic then it might as well be hers.

Maybe she'd misjudged him earlier. And maybe, in spite of his professional success and reserved manner, he was a generous man.

His next statement proved her wrong.

'Before you label me with all sorts of altruistic motives—don't. I'm afraid my help will be rather short term,' he said. 'Six months at the most. Perhaps by then you'll have found a physician's assistant.'

Hilda's comment about slumming resurfaced, creating

a new concern. 'The people who come to this clinic are as important as those who can afford to go to yours. I won't have them treated as charity cases,' she warned.

'Did I imply otherwise?' His voice was cool.

'As long as we understand each other. By the way, the salary isn't much.' Bracing herself for a hoot of laughter or a sneer, she quoted a figure equal to her own wages.

The corners of his mouth turned upward, the closest she'd seen to a true smile. The planes of his face softened, revealing a faint pattern of crow's feet near his eyes. 'Trying to change my mind, Dr Holloway?'

'No,' she said, her tone as stiff as her spine. 'Just pointing out the facts.'

'Good. I'm not here for the salary, anyway, so the size of it doesn't matter.' He shrugged. 'Might as well keep it.'

'Keep it?' she parroted, dumbfounded.

He nodded. 'Apply it to whatever you need—baby formula, medicine, new wallpaper—I don't care.'

Kirsten stared at him. Would this man always act contrary to her expectations? Yet she, like her patients, had her pride and the sooner Dr Marshall realized it the better. A deadly calm filled her voice.

'A mother brought her son today for a check-up. She was thrilled to pay me one dollar because in the past she couldn't afford a single dime. Even though her contribution didn't come *close* to paying for the service she received we accepted it with grace in order to preserve her dignity. Just because we can't pay you what you're worth I won't have it bandied about the medical community that I took advantage of you.'

He held up his hands. 'I get the picture. I'll be happy

to accept the salary you've quoted.' He paused. 'So?
Am I hired?'

Leery of the situation, she wanted to say no. Like her
predecessor, she wanted someone who was motivated to
help these people out of the goodness of his heart—
someone who would be willing to agree to a long-term
commitment. A physician who only wanted to fulfill
an old obligation—one who wouldn't let the door hit
his backside when his duty had been met—didn't
measure up.

Unfortunately, no one else had applied for the position, much less met her criteria. No one, except Jakob
Marshall.

Even though she didn't think he'd last the six months
he'd mentioned, fate had supplied the proverbial gift
horse. Desperate, she couldn't afford the luxury of
inspecting it too closely.

She forced a smile. 'Welcome aboard.'

Kirsten rose, ready to seal their agreement with a
handshake, but a harsh pounding on the back door caught
her attention. Instinct predicted an emergency.

Without a word, she turned and ran along the corridor.
Flinging open the door, she ignored the blast of cold
wind against her body.

She recognized the seven-year-old dark-haired girl
and her ten-year-old brother, fidgeting on the step. Both
wore ill-fitting jackets at least one size too big, knitted
stocking caps and mufflers.

'You gotta come,' Davey said, sounding frantic as his
eyes reflected his fear. 'Grampa is real sick. His chest
hurts and the pills he's been takin' aren't helpin'.'

'Come inside while I get my coat.'

The two children obeyed without argument, and she
closed the door behind them. Hurrying down the hall-

way, she retraced her steps and met Jakob outside her office.

'What's wrong?' he asked.

She sidestepped him to grab her parka and medical bag. 'Sixty-year-old with possible unstable angina,' she said, thrusting her arms into the sleeves. 'I've treated him in the past with nitroglycerin, but it sounds as if it's not working. I'm heading over there.'

Jakob reached for his coat. 'We'll take my Jeep,' he said as he strode alongside her to the exit.

Kirsten stopped in her tracks, surprised by his take-charge attitude after being employed less than five minutes.

He looked over his shoulder at her. 'Would you rather handle this by yourself? This *is* my area of expertise.'

For an instant she'd forgotten their agreement to defer to the more experienced member of the team as the situation warranted. If Harry Tanner's angina had progressed to a more serious condition it would be nice to have a cardiologist's opinion. Hurrying to catch up to him, she said, 'Fine. He's all yours.'

The four of them piled into his vehicle, with Davey supplying the directions to their house. Once Kirsten had the address she dialed the emergency number and requested an ambulance.

The ride to the Tanner apartment took less than five minutes. Jakob screeched to a halt in front of the building and shifted into park mode.

The young girl, Lucy, hopped out of the Jeep and slipped to her knees on a patch of ice. Without breaking stride, Jakob hoisted her up and carried her into the complex. Davey led the way to their second-floor apartment.

At the top of the stairs the children's mother, Maggie,

and a man who also appeared to be in his late thirties, met them. 'Thank God you've come,' she declared, ushering the group through their small living quarters and into her father's bedroom.

Harry Tanner sat against the headboard, with pillows cushioning his back. His face was pale and beaded with sweat. 'Don't know why she called you over my indigestion. Danged black-eyed peas do it ever' time.'

Maggie cut him off, speaking quickly to prevent her father from interrupting. 'He's complained of chest pain, going down his arms and back and up into his neck and jaw. It's lasted for a long time and his pills aren't working. The past few weeks his attacks have seemed to come on more often too. I've tried to bring him to see you, but he wouldn't co-operate.'

'I can talk for myself,' Harry muttered.

Kirsten dropped her coat onto a chair and approached the bed. 'I brought Dr Marshall along to give us his opinion. He's a heart specialist who'll be working at the clinic for a while.'

'Suit yourself. But it's only—' Harry's breath caught and at the same moment he clutched at his chest.

Kirsten moved closer, noticing that Jakob did the same.

'Hurts...bad,' Harry managed to say before he slumped sideways.

Immediately Kirsten checked the carotid artery in his neck. 'No pulse,' she called out. She yanked away the pillows while Jakob pulled on Harry's feet to straighten the elderly man's body. Working together, they rolled Harry over until he lay flat on his back.

Jakob began CPR, counting each chest compression. Kirsten tipped Harry's head back, ready to breathe into Harry's lungs when Jakob reached five. 'Davey,' she said, 'watch for the ambulance, please.'

The youngster glided out of the room like a shadow. His mother stood at the foot of the bed, with her companion's comforting arm around her shoulders.

Time dragged on. Knowing the amount of energy expended and sensing Jakob's growing exhaustion, Kirsten nudged his arm. 'Let me take over for a while.'

He let her. Placing her hands on the man's chest, she fell into Jakob's previously established rhythm. 'I'd think. . .the paramedics. . .should be here. . .by now,' she puffed.

Jakob checked the man's carotid pulse. 'They'd better have a damn good reason for the delay.'

Footsteps and voices heralded the arrival of a police officer and two EMS staff. 'About time,' Jakob retorted. 'We need oxygen and an EKG. Get the paddles ready.'

Kirsten relinquished her spot and duties to a technician, who attached the leads to Harry's chest with a speed born out of experience and urgency. The EKG readout showed a flat line and Jakob applied the defibrillator paddles to the man's chest. 'Clear.'

The wavy blip didn't appear.

Jakob repeated the procedure. Again the monitor's line stayed straight. He spouted more orders and the EMTs complied with well-orchestrated movements. Minutes passed. Epinephrine and a host of other measures proved ineffectual.

Soon the outcome became obvious. Jakob glanced at Kirsten and she nodded her agreement. They'd done all they could.

Kirsten moved to Maggie's side. 'I'm sorry,' she murmured. In the background the EMTs packed their equipment, the latches of their suitcase-sized drug box and defibrillator snapping with crisp finality.

Maggie hiccuped and wiped away the tears streaming down her face. With one arm around Lucy, she nodded and whispered, 'Thanks for coming.'

The man standing nearby introduced himself. 'I'm Lew, their neighbor. I'll help her make the arrangements.'

'Good.' Kirsten addressed Maggie. 'If you need anything, please let me know.'

The woman bobbed her head.

Lucy tugged on Kirsten's sleeve. 'Grampa turned the jump rope for me today,' she said, her eyes brimming with tears. 'Mama said he wasn't s'posed to, but we sneaked downstairs so's he could. Did that make him die?'

The child's misery sent a sharp pain into Kirsten's chest. The exercise probably hadn't helped his angina but his history suggested that his heart had been on the verge of a myocardial infarction. Regardless of the contributing factors, it was all academic now. Harry was gone. Her concern was for the living, and she refused to let this child assume responsibility for an old man's death.

She hunkered down to Lucy's eye level and hugged her. 'Oh, sweetie, your grandfather's heart was tired and worn out. It wasn't your fault.'

Kirsten stroked Lucy's hair. 'You and Davey were very brave to come for us. I'm sure your mom is proud of you.'

'Then he didn't die 'cause of me?'

Kirsten shook her head. 'No, and don't ever think that. OK?'

'OK,' Lucy whispered, moving into her mother's outstretched arms to share an embrace with her brother.

Kirsten rose and Jakob helped her into her coat. They

left the apartment and descended the steps at a more leisurely pace. This time Kirsten noticed the smell of a variety of foods—beef stew near one door, a chocolate cake by another. The combination made her stomach grumble, reminding her of the late hour. Even so, the mundane odors seemed out of place with the scent of death lingering in her nostrils.

Once outside she inhaled the crisp air and cleared her throat. The north wind's sting to her unprotected skin diverted the pain in her heart over losing a patient.

As if aware of her inner distress, Jakob placed a comforting hand under her elbow and guided her to his Jeep just as the EMTs brought Harry's body outside.

Kirsten watched them load the gurney and slam the double doors. 'I wish he had come to me a few weeks ago. Maybe I could have done something.'

'Maybe. Maybe not.' At her questioning look he added, 'You did what you could. Put it behind you.'

'Sort of a cynical, hard-hearted attitude, wouldn't you say?' she asked.

'No. It's being objective. As much as we'd like it to, our profession doesn't come with any guarantees.'

She stared at the ambulance now pulling away and focused on the red tail-lights blinking in the darkness. 'I still wish we could have saved him.' She took a deep breath. 'I want all the Harry Tanners in the world to know that help is available. They don't need to stay at home and suffer. Or die prematurely.'

'It's hard to change the habits and mindset of a lifetime.'

'I have to try.'

Jakob started the engine and drove toward the clinic. 'Are you this personally involved with all of your clients?'

The question, so reminiscent of the one her ex-fiancé had asked before their relationship had begun to disintegrate, raised warning flags in her mind. Although Jakob didn't speak in Edward's patronizing manner, she stiffened her spine, squared her shoulders and prepared for verbal battle.

'Shouldn't I get *involved*?'

He kept his attention on the road. 'It depends.'

'I'm afraid I missed the lecture on "Distancing Yourself from Your Patient",' Kirsten said with a trace of acid in her tone. 'I'm sure you can recite it verbatim, but I don't care to hear it.'

His voice was equally sharp. 'I asked a simple question, requiring a simple answer. No offense was intended. Believe it or not, I didn't bring up the subject to start a debate or to pass judgement.'

'Oh, really?' Even though he'd denied it she sensed that he'd labelled her as another woman with her head in the clouds, unsuited to the harshness and emotional demands of this profession.

'I wondered if you had a soft spot for this particular family. That's all.'

Suitably chastized, she bit her lip—conscious of Jakob's masculine scent permeating the interior of the vehicle. 'I take a personal interest in everyone who depends on me for their medical care.'

He nodded, as if she'd confirmed the opinion he'd already derived. No doubt he thought her as foolish as Edward had. A specialist, interested only in a particular body part or organ system, wouldn't understand her concern about the person as a whole.

'Since we'll be working together,' he began, 'it's important that we know each other's strengths and weaknesses. We have to establish common ground in order to make the next few months tolerable for both of us.'

Although his comment made sense it occurred to her that, in spite of his insistence to join her in the practice, he, too, had reservations about their working arrangement.

A host of questions hovered in the back of her mind, but before she could voice them he drove into the parking lot behind her clinic and braked next to her ten-year-old Pontiac. Leaving the motor running, he said, 'I'll see you on Tuesday.'

They may have held opposing views, but it wasn't cause for rudeness. She thrust out her right hand. 'Thanks for the ride.'

'Glad to help.' He grasped her fingers. His warm skin chased away the chill deep in her bones, filling her with an odd sense of excitement. Unnerved by her instantaneous reaction, she pulled away. This couldn't happen—she wouldn't allow it. Intimate relationships with close colleagues did not work out.

The urge to rescind her job offer grew stronger but reason prevented her from taking action. She dug in her coat pocket and extracted a sturdy metal ring, holding a variety of keys. Twisting one loose and taking care not to touch him, she dropped it into his palm. 'Before I forget, you'll need this. It unlocks the back door.'

For a few seconds Jakob stared at the object, before closing his fist around it. 'My employment is now official, isn't it?'

Kirsten couldn't tell if he was elated or disappointed. 'Unless tonight's episode has scared you off.'

He shifted position to drop the key in the side pocket of his trousers. With an uplifted eyebrow, he stared at her. 'Expecting me to quit so soon?'

She shrugged. 'Stranger things have happened.'

'If that's a challenge, I accept. It will take more than a few house calls to change my plans, Kirsten.' Her name rolled off his tongue slowly, like gooey caramel dripping down a Red Delicious apple.

'I'm glad to hear it. Jakob.' His name had a pleasant ring and she'd enjoyed saying it more than she thought she should. Troubled by her perceived weakness, she opened the door and hopped down to plant both feet on the pavement.

'Kirsten?' His softened baritone captured her attention.

She hesitated, shivering with each bite of the sharp, night air through her clothing. The glow from the interior light made the silver streaks in his hair shine. 'Yes?'

'I prefer to be called Jake.'

'I'll remember.'

'Oh, and Kirsten?'

Her teeth chattered. 'Yeah?'

'Happy New Year.'

The next afternoon Jake stood in front of the blaze burning in his fireplace and tapped another golf ball to the far corner of the room. It missed the regulation-sized putting cup and banged into two others lying in its path. All three rolled in different directions and thudded against the floorboards. Scowling over his poor aim and frustrated by his failure, he tugged at the collar of his multicolored rugby shirt. A button flew off and his mood grew darker.

Two dozen balls of various colors cluttered the floor, causing his carpet to resemble a giant billiards table rather than a makeshift golfing green. How pathetic for a thirty-nine-year-old man to spend the holiday attempting a simple three-yard putt.

He assumed his stance and tapped another ball toward its imitation hole. The small globe rolled around the outer edge but, instead of falling in, shot off course. Damn! Another stroke.

Logs shifted in a flurry of sparks as the fire crackled and popped. The smell of burning wood drifted toward him, creating an atmosphere so similar to the one last Sunday when he'd visited his grandparents. . .

'Your father's trust fund is gone,' Jakob had told his grandfather, Ian Marshall.

The elderly Scotsman had sucked in his breath. 'What do you mean, "gone"?'

'The accountant forged our signatures and withdrew the money.'

Ian had reached for his favorite pipe, appearing stunned. 'Why did he do such a thing?'

'Steve has a problem with gambling. According to the police, we won't ever see the money again.'

In the ensuing quiet Jake had watched Ian chew on the mouthpiece of his pipe. Although his grandfather had given up his tobacco some time ago, he still clung to the motions of his old habit.

The silence stretched on and Jake felt compelled to break it. 'Charges have been filed and he's in jail at the moment.' He hesitated. 'I'm sorry, Gramps.'

Ian waved his pipe in the air. 'It's not your fault.'

'I hired him.'

'So the famous cardiologist thinks he can see into a man's heart?' Ian asked, raising one shaggy white eyebrow.

Jake smiled. Although technology had made the feat possible, his grandfather wasn't referring to the physical ability. 'I'd like to think so. You can.'

'I'm seventy-nine years old, Jakob. My knowledge of people didn't come by accident. I've made mistakes, many of them. Some I could correct, others I couldn't.' He paused. 'The fund was an investment for us, but we can survive without it. However, those who benefited from its earnings may not.'

Jakob nodded. 'According to the original terms of the trust, recipients must receive a termination notice. I've already authorized the bank to notify the Family Health Center and, as per great-grandfather's clause, I'll help with the most pressing needs over the next six months.'

'Those terms were established to prevent any of the Marshall descendants from misusing the money. You don't have to go to these lengths.'

'Yes, I do,' Jake insisted.

'You really *want* to do this?'

He shrugged. 'You placed me in charge of our business affairs—therefore, I'm ultimately responsible.'

Ian smiled. 'Somehow I'm not surprised that you feel this way.' He tucked his pipe back into his mouth. 'How will you handle the situation?'

'I've issued a check to cover this quarter's usual amount, which the bank will include with their letter. I also intend to visit Dr Holloway. In the future she may prefer equipment or supplies instead of money.'

Ian paused. 'And if she asks for something else?'

Jake dismissed the idea. 'Not likely.'

Jake shook his head, still amazed at how his best-laid plans had gone awry. Expecting to pay for his sins with the scratch of a pen, he'd never dreamed that he'd have to make restitution with something he couldn't afford to give—his time. Yet he was bound by his principles— he wouldn't wriggle out of his responsibilities.

The doorbell interrupted his musing. Leaning his club against a chair, instinct told him before he reached the front entrance who had come to visit.

'Happy New Year, Jakob.' White-haired Matilda Marshall bustled into Jake's foyer with an energy surpassing that of most of her contemporaries.

'Same to you, Grams.' He bent to hug her stocky frame.

'Our German tradition is for children to visit their elders on New Year's Day,' she scolded without malice. 'Not the other way around.'

His railroad clock bonged three times, saving him from a reply. Before the noise had faded Jake had hung her coat on the three-legged coatrack and had led her into his den.

Moving to the fireplace, she warmed her hands. 'I can't get over how much your study resembles Ian's, right down to the clipper ship on the mantel.'

He let the comment pass. He'd loved his grandfather's room and had spent many happy hours there, especially after his parents had died.

'He is expecting you,' she chided.

Jake kneaded the back of his neck. 'I've been busy trying to wrap up some paperwork.'

Matilda glanced first at his cluttered desk, then at the golf balls scattered across the floor. 'So I see.'

She grabbed the putter and tapped a fluorescent pink ball toward the cup. It rolled in with ease. 'You've been working for a long time. You must have accomplished a lot.'

He grinned. 'You know me too well.'

Her lined face lit up. She returned the club to its previous position, before settling herself into an easy chair. 'You are like Ian. He always weighed things in his mind while he golfed. After he taught you the game you fell into the same pattern. That hasn't changed, has it?'

'No.' Jake sat in the stuffed chair opposite hers.

'Did you go to the Family Health Center?'

He nodded. 'Our meeting didn't turn out quite the way I'd anticipated.'

'Oh?'

'Although Dr Holloway can use the money she wants a doctor instead.'

'And you will be that doctor,' Matilda guessed.

'Yes,' he said ruefully. Kirsten Holloway's business inexperience and idealism made the situation he found himself in a more bitter pill to swallow.

'You know, Jakob, you don't have to go through with this,' she said gently, repeating Ian's earlier assurances. 'We don't hold you responsible.'

He smiled a lopsided grin. 'You may not, but I do.'

'You're busy with remodeling your own clinic,' Matilda protested. 'And you run yourself ragged now. How will you manage?'

Although the question preyed on his mind, he sought to reassure her. 'The other two physicians in my office, Roy and Scott, will cover while I'm unavailable. It should work out.' He rose, reaching for the putter.

She visibly relaxed. 'Everything happens for a purpose.'

'That may be, but at the moment I can't see any divine plan.' He tapped a ball and watched it miss the mark by several inches. 'In fact, the only thing I foresee is that the clinic can't stay open much longer.'

'I hope you're wrong. I'd hate for Frank Morrison's work to end. So would your grandfather. So,' she said in a tone that brooked no argument, 'tell me about this Dr Holloway.'

Jake pinched the bridge of his nose, hating it when his grandmother enquired about the women he met. 'Considering her for the role of granddaughter-in-law?'

'Who can guess what will happen? Especially since she'll spend so much time with you.'

'It won't be that often.'

'Still, I want to know.' Matilda's face took on a stubbornness that Jake recognized.

Leaning against his desk, he pressed his lips together as he brought his memory into focus. 'She's in her late twenties, about average height, nice-looking, reddish-brown hair to here.' He pointed to his chin.

At the same time Kirsten's sensual mouth and the graceful sway to her hips flashed into his mental picture. Those, however, were observations better left unmentioned, especially to his grandmother.

Jake paused. 'I've never seen eyes like hers before.'

'What do you mean?'

'One's blue and the other is sort of blue-green. You don't notice it at first, but when you do it's fascinating.' He smiled. 'When she's angry the colors become more intense.'

'She has a temper?' Matilda's voice sounded pained.

'Not at all. It's more like she's protective.'

'Ah.' The distaste on her face cleared. 'So you think you can work with her?'

The idealist and the cynic—a volatile combination, if he'd ever heard of one. Even two days a week could prove to be too much to handle.

He assumed his stance, gauged the distance and tapped his final ball. It hit the edge of the cup, then dropped inside with a clank. 'I don't have a choice, do I?'

CHAPTER THREE

JAKE'S arrival on the following Tuesday was like a double-edged sword. Kirsten found the slower pace both enjoyable and worrisome. After all, he hadn't worked in a family practice for a long time. What if he missed something?

The suspense grew for several hours until, finally, she cornered Amy. 'How's he doing?'

Amy frowned. 'Who? The patient or Dr Marshall?'

Kirsten grinned, unwilling to admit that she was checking up on her own colleague. 'Both.'

'Mr Rawlings definitely has problems. Dr Marshall found a small lump in his prostate.'

'Did he order lab work?'

Amy nodded. 'Plus a consult with a urologist. Irene is making the arrangements now.'

'Good.'

'As for Dr Marshall, he's doing as well as can be expected.'

Kirsten tapped one shoe on the floor. 'I'm not interested in a press report. I want to know—'

Amy shrugged. 'He's fine. Seems to be thorough.'

A portion of Kirsten's tension disappeared. 'What a relief.'

'I'm sure he'll warm up to the patients as time goes on. Then again,' Amy mused, tapping an index finger against her cheek, 'maybe it's his way of doing things.'

'No bedside manner, hmm?' Figures, she thought. A heart doctor without heart.

Amy appeared uncomfortable. 'I wouldn't exactly say that. He's, well, polite, but he projects an all-business attitude. Doesn't make small talk, if you know what I mean.'

'I see.'

'Working into a new routine is tough. But I'm sure once he learns the ropes and our patients he'll relax.'

Kirsten doubted it. Jake seemed to possess more characteristics of a Type A personality than its opposite. As a cardiologist, he should know better. 'Would you be as generous with your patience if he were short, fifty pounds overweight and ugly?'

'Probably not,' Amy said, her voice cheerful. 'I think it's wonderful that such a busy man is willing to spend time here with us. He's one of a kind.'

'You bet he is,' Kirsten replied, tongue in cheek.

'Rich, successful, handsome in that brooding sort of way.' Amy's face took on a dreamy expression. 'What more could a woman want?'

'I can think of a few things.'

Kirsten's wry tone obviously caught Amy's attention. 'I thought you wanted a second doctor on staff.'

'A family practitioner, not a specialist.'

'If you don't like him why hire him?'

How could she explain that she despised what he represented—the highly successful upper echelon of the medical community—and not the man himself?

'It's not that I don't like him,' Kirsten said. 'I'm just not sure about his motives, that's all. He came to me with a story about fulfilling some obligation and, since we're desperate, I couldn't say no.' She shrugged. 'But he'll do.'

Crumpling a note she'd scribbled to herself the day before, Kirsten glanced at her watch. She might have time to straighten the drug cabinet before lunch.

'There's more to it than that, isn't there?' Amy asked. 'I don't think I've ever seen you as tense as you've been today.'

Kirsten straightened her shoulders and fluffed her bangs. 'I'm not tense.' Seeing Amy's dubious expression, she forced a smile. 'Maybe a little.'

'A little overprotective toward your patients, Dr Holloway?' Amy teased.

Kirsten clutched at Amy's perfect excuse and this time Kirsten's smile came freely. 'I suppose. You'll keep me posted if something comes up?'

Amy nodded. 'You bet.' She moved toward the patient room she'd left a few minutes earlier. 'Gotta go. Dr Marshall might need some help.'

Somewhat appeased by Amy's comments, Kirsten strode to the drug closet and began to organize its contents. Immersed in her project, time passed quickly.

'I'm impressed.' Jake's voice came from behind.

Startled, she twirled. 'Oh?'

He pointed to the pharmaceuticals. 'I found potassium tablets next to the antifungal cream. Since then I've been trying to figure out your system. I'm usually good at piecing clues together but you have me stumped. Did you design it to confuse would-be thieves?'

'It wouldn't be worth the effort. They usually steal everything we have.'

'How often have you been robbed?' He sounded incredulous.

She squinted while she thought. 'We haven't been robbed in over a year. Word must have gotten out that we don't have anything of street value.'

'What makes you say that?' He propped one shoulder against the wall.

She met his gaze. 'We only had suppositories in stock the last time they broke in. Before that, they got a few bottles of prenatal vitamins. It wasn't worth their effort.'

'Not unless they were constipated or pregnant.'

She laughed. 'True.'

'Will you teach me your system or do I have to muddle through on my own?' His voice held a note of humor.

Kirsten turned around and began to arrange the boxes into neat rows. 'Much as I hate to shatter your image, I must confess. After we received the meds yesterday no one had time to put them away. Today, I do.'

Jake leaned closer to peer inside. 'I see. What a relief to find antibiotics in their proper place. Now I won't have to rummage through everything to find what I want.'

'I'd appreciate it if you'd mark the sheet I have posted whenever you use the supplies. That way our shopping list is ready at a moment's notice.'

'No problem.'

With his head close to hers, Kirsten could smell his cologne. Although she didn't recognize the brand, whatever it was fitted him as no other men's fragrance could. Anything that smooth, that exotic, had to be expensive and guaranteed to attract women like ants to sugar. From the pounding of her heart, she apparently wasn't an exception.

Focus on business, she reprimanded herself. 'Things going well?'

'Yeah. Of course I haven't had anything difficult— sore throats, coughs, a skin rash. Pretty basic for someone who's a little rusty.'

His grin revealed straight white teeth, although one of his top incisors had a chipped edge—something she hadn't noticed before. In the light of today's congeniality the imperfection made him seem more approachable.

She opened her mouth, ready to extend an invitation to share lunch, but Irene interrupted.

'Dr Marshall. You have a call on line two. A Roy Erickson.'

Jake stiffened and his entire demeanor changed. The smile lines around his mouth disappeared. His eyes narrowed, transforming him into the serious, no-nonsense physician she was most familiar with. 'Thanks.' He turned on one heel and strode toward his temporary office which happened to be close to hers.

'Bad news, I'll bet,' Irene remarked.

Kirsten watched him disappear down the hall, sorry to see the relaxed version of Dr Marshall go—the version she found both stimulating and captivating. 'Could be.'

A few minutes later he reappeared, all traces of his earlier humor gone. 'I have to leave.'

'Problems?' she asked, closing the cabinet door now that she'd completed her task.

'Yes. My partner called. I'm not sure when I'll be back. Barring unforeseen complications. . .' he glanced at his Rolex watch '. . .it may be around three.'

Assuming that he had a patient who had gone sour, she sympathized. 'Don't worry. I can manage for a few hours.'

Relief flickered in his eyes. 'I hate to dump my share of the work on you so soon, but this meeting with my new accountant is important.'

He's meeting his *accountant*? she thought, dazed by his announcement. Then she swallowed, wishing she could take back her magnanimous gesture. How typical with men of his ilk—drop needy patients in favor of stocks, bonds and investment strategy.

Squaring her shoulders, she added, with a note to

her voice as frosty as the air outside, 'Of course.'

Without giving him another glance, she marched into her office, pulled a carton of blueberry yogurt out of the table-top refrigerator and plunked it on her desk. To think that those few minutes of camaraderie had nearly caused her to revise her jaded opinion of him. Hah!

Amy entered a few minutes later. 'I saw Dr Marshall leaving. Didn't he want to eat with us?'

'I didn't get a chance to ask. He was too busy hurrying to a meeting with his *accountant*.'

Amy's mouth formed an O to match the size of her eyes. 'When will he be back?'

Kirsten shrugged. 'Who knows?'

'But what will I do with the patients? We double-booked today because we knew there would be two of you.'

'Have Irene reschedule anyone who doesn't want to wait. Otherwise, plan on working overtime,' Kirsten advised.

As if sensing Kirsten's mood, Amy fell silent. An hour later, when their doors opened for the afternoon, a steady stream of people poured in. Soon the waiting area had standing room only while Kirsten bustled from one case to another.

Her opinion of Jake sank lower and lower with each passing hour. Surely a meeting to discuss finances didn't take all afternoon!

'Something else may have come up.' Amy defended Jake, apparently noticing Kirsten's growing ire.

'Then he could have telephoned.' Kirsten grabbed a chart hanging from the wall outside room three. Taking a calming breath, she went inside.

'It's my leg again,' Mick Peters blurted the moment Kirsten appeared.

The overweight forty-five-year-old construction worker's lower right leg was swollen to nearly twice its normal size. The superficial veins were prominent and his skin was warm to the touch.

'It hurts bad.'

'How long has it been like this?' she asked.

'Started this morning. By noon it had swollen so much I thought my jeans would pop. I went home to change pants and came right here.'

'I'm going to admit you to the hospital. I'm fairly certain you have a deep vein thrombosis.'

He winced. 'I was afraid you'd say that. Can't I just stay home, take my medicine and—?'

'Absolutely not. You know from your last episode. . .' she checked his record '. . .nine months ago that this is a very serious condition. The clot in your vein may or may not have completely blocked off the blood flow. In addition, it could break off and travel to one of your lungs, creating even worse problems.'

'I can't afford to be off work.'

'You don't have a choice. Go to the KU Medical Center immediately—don't run home and get your toothbrush, either. We'll run a venogram, do a few lab tests and start you on heparin right away.'

He frowned. 'I suppose.'

'Do you need to call your wife?'

'Nah, she's in the waiting-room.'

Kirsten nodded. 'Then the sooner you get there the better. I'll check in on you this evening.' With that, she left to make the arrangements.

By the time the waiting room had emptied both the sun and her part-time billing clerk had been gone for at least two hours.

'What a day,' Kirsten said, collapsing in her office. She kicked off her loafers to massage her aching feet. 'Tomorrow has to be better.'

'I hope so.' Amy unwrapped a chocolate bar as she plopped into another chair. Taking a bite, she closed her eyes. 'Mmm, this is good.'

Kirsten popped open a can of cola. 'Is that your supper?'

Amy broke off the other end. 'It's my appetizer. Want some?'

Kirsten reached across her desk and took the portion Amy handed her. 'Thanks.'

'I'll stop and get something nutritious from MacDonald's on the way home. The drive-up lady recognizes me by my voice and my order—a chef salad with Ranch dressing and a chocolate milk shake.'

Kirsten chewed her bite-sized snack in silence, too exhausted to make conversation.

Amy drained her cup of water in one gulp. 'What do you suppose Dr Marshall is doing now?'

Kirsten shrugged. 'Probably relaxing at home, sipping something imported while he soaks in his hot tub and worries over which mutual fund will yield the greatest return.'

Sitting in the doctors' changing-room, Jake pulled the green surgical cap off his head and leaned against the wall. A cold beer sounded good right now but, since he was on call, it would have to wait.

He'd been on the go ever since the interview with Barry Morgan. It had only taken two hours to outline his plans and discuss his expectations, but two emergency calls from St Luke's had prevented his return to Kirsten's clinic.

Kirsten. Closing his eyes, he recalled her easy smile, full of sunshine and warmth—something in short supply these cold January days. Even her fresh clean scent reminded him of spring. But spring days had rain and at one point a cloud had appeared on her face.

Although he'd recognized her immediate withdrawal once he'd disclosed his reasons for leaving he couldn't understand why she'd reacted so strongly. Given enough time, though—six months, to be exact—he would. Meanwhile, he'd have to make up for skipping out on her.

His secretary loved roses or a potted plant. Although Kirsten would probably enjoy them as well—the clown and the picture of a Ferris wheel lit against a night sky, which decorated her office, suggested that she had a carefree side—those things didn't seem quite right for this situation. She'd appreciate something more practical, he decided, perhaps something for the clinic.

The door swung open and his assistant, Scott Rydell, entered. He sat next to Jake on the hard bench. 'Meier's vital signs are stable and he's resting comfortably.'

Jake wiped his face with a towel. 'You did a good job. It won't be long until you're on your own.'

Scott's fair complexion turned ruddy. 'Thanks. Performing an angioplasty is rather nerve-racking.'

Jake grinned. 'Threading a catheter into an artery and inflating a balloon to stretch the narrowed section isn't totally a stress-free procedure, no matter how many you've done. Experience cuts down on the number of complications, but you never know if this is the patient who will be the exception.'

'Hopefully, Meier won't be one of them.' Scott rose. 'I'll monitor him for a little longer before I leave.'

'Page me if you need anything.' Jake straightened,

flexing his shoulders as he glanced at the wall clock. 'Looks like I'll make it to the spa before they close for the night.'

Scott's jaw dropped. 'You're going to exercise?'

'No. I'm going to soak in the Jacuzzi. See you tomorrow.'

The younger doctor had one foot outside the room when Jake had an idea. He called out, 'Hey, Scott? Didn't you pack up a box of drug samples when we cleaned out the office a few days ago?'

'Yeah. It's mostly meds we don't use so I planned to toss them. Why?'

'Are they still good?'

'There might be a few outdated units but most of it is OK.'

'I'll take whatever you've got.'

Scott grinned. 'Starting your own pharmacy on the side? I thought with your latest project you wouldn't have time to take on another.'

'You're right, I don't, but Dr Holloway might be able to use the supplies. Her patients at the health center are always desperate for medicine.'

'Dr Holloway? *Kirsten* Holloway?' Scott asked.

Jake nodded. 'You know her?'

'Sort of. She was a year behind me in med school. Looked too young and defenseless for the rigorous training, but underneath it all she was smart, dedicated and had a steel backbone. I sat next to her at a lecture once and she mentioned how much she enjoyed working at the inner city clinics.'

Jake wasn't surprised.

'At the time I assumed she'd work there, even though she had a lot of job offers. Apparently, my guess was fairly close.' Scott paused. 'Is she married?'

Jake pictured her hands as she had performed CPR. Her fingers had been bare, which didn't necessarily mean anything. 'I don't think so.'

Scott's eyes gleamed, his interest unmistakable. 'If you ever need someone to fill in for you, let me know. I wouldn't mind renewing old acquaintances, if you catch my drift.' He wiggled his sandy-colored eyebrows.

Jake did. Both to his astonishment and his dismay, he didn't like the idea. 'I'll keep it in mind, but I have a feeling your *boss* will run you ragged. You won't have time for socializing. Not for a while.'

'Probably not.' Scott reopened the door. 'I'll have the box on your desk first thing in the morning.'

Alone again, Jake stripped off his shirt. The medical supplies would be appreciated, but he needed something else. . . An idea came to him and he grinned. It was the perfect peace offering.

'Sorry I'm late.' A week later Kirsten rushed out of her office, tugging her lab coat over her teal silk blouse and gray trousers. 'Susan Lightfoot's baby took her sweet time in making her appearance.'

'No problem,' Amy announced. 'Dr Marshall has been working like a trouper.'

Kirsten's hands stilled over a button. 'So he finally made it.'

'Eight o'clock. On the dot.'

Kirsten let out a breath and finished sliding the button through the hole. 'Then I'm not as far behind as I'd thought.'

'As a matter of fact, we're right on schedule and everything's under control. By the way, Irene stuck a few messages on your desk.'

'OK. Call if you need me.'

Back at her desk, Kirsten was suddenly at a loss. After running at full speed for so long, she didn't know how to switch gears. Ever since Jake had canceled on Thursday she hadn't expected to see him again—obligation or not. But he had returned so she intended to take advantage of the freedom he had given her.

Gazing at her pile of phone messages and the stacks of mail and journals, she replanned her morning and set to work. Close to one o'clock she sensed a presence in the doorway and glanced up from the article on sexually transmitted diseases.

Jake lounged against the frame, his white-jacketed arms folded across his chest. The Windsor knot of his red and navy silk tie showed above the V of his lab coat neckline, giving him an elegant air. 'I hear you had a delivery.'

Contrasting his classy clothing with her own off-the-rack outfit, she decided that, in more ways than one, he was as out of place in her center as an angelfish in a bowl of guppies. 'A healthy girl, thank goodness.'

'Were you expecting problems?'

'No, but one never knows. Besides, after three sons, my patient was determined to have a daughter. I'm glad she got her wish before they ended up with a brood rivaling the Vienna Boys' Choir.'

'I'd like to—' A loud buzzer went off and Kirsten jumped to her feet. 'What's wrong?' he asked.

'Trouble,' she said, darting past him. 'That's Irene's signal.'

Kirsten rushed down the corridor. Out of the corner of one eye she saw Amy fall in behind Jake. Angry voices grew louder as she approached the waiting-room, where a group of teenage boys had congregated. Two of them—battered, bruised and bloodied, but still in the fighting spirit—were being held apart by their comrades.

Kirsten glanced at Jake. He had distaste written across his face. No doubt he was busy comparing the social skills of *his* patients to hers, and hers were coming up short. Eager to end the scene, she stepped forward.

'Cut it out, guys,' she ordered. No one paid any attention.

'You cheated, man,' the dark-haired Mexican youth accused, his ponytail swaying with each swing of his fist.

'I did not,' the light-haired one with his head shaved military style retorted. 'I won fair and square.'

'Don't lie to me. My buddies saw you.'

Grunts, heated words and curses flowed freely from both sides, filling the air until Kirsten couldn't hear herself think. She held out her hand and Irene dropped a referee's whistle into her palm.

Amy leaned closer to Jake. 'Get ready.'

Kirsten blew a steady blast, long enough to make everyone stop and cover their ears.

'Good job, Doctor,' Jake murmured. 'You missed your calling. Should have been with riot control.'

'I've had plenty of practice,' she muttered back, returning the small but powerful attention-getter to Irene. With her shoulders stiff, she stepped into the fray.

'You,' Kirsten commanded, pointing to the Mexican boy in the torn flannel shirt. Each rip in the fabric revealed a bleeding line, and one eye was starting to swell. 'What's your name?'

'Alfonso Rodriguez.'

'Alfonso, go with Dr Marshall.'

She turned to the other. 'And you are?'

'Lonnie Turner.'

'OK, Lonnie, you come with me. Two of you stay here to take Lonnie and Alfonso home. The rest of you had better leave before I call the cops. Got that?'

Four boys, ranging in size, age and ethnic background, nodded and scampered to the door. The other two sprawled in chairs on opposite sides of the room.

While Amy and Dr Marshall tended to one boy Kirsten dealt with the other. 'What happened?' she asked Lonnie, who was about sixteen.

He made a face as he pulled off the tattered remnants of his shirt, sliced in the same manner as Alfonso's. His lip was split and a small cut, probably delivered by a ring, graced his cheek-bone.

'We were playing poker during our lunch hour. He thought I dealt from the bottom of the deck but I didn't.'

'Must have been high stakes,' she commented, examining the deep gashes on the boy's arms and torso. She pulled on a pair of gloves and opened a sterile suture pack.

'Fifty bucks. Anyways, Alfonso starts throwing punches. Next thing I know he grabs this old whiskey bottle off the ground and breaks it. Then he comes after me. I had to defend myself.'

'Well, I don't know about Alfonso but you're going to need stitches.' She glanced over his bare chest, seeing several white lines of scar tissue criss-crossing his pale skin.

'Looks like this has happened before.'

He grimaced as she injected a local anesthetic in several places. 'Once or twice.'

Lonnie bore her ministrations in silence. Finally, she tied the last knot. Moving to his face, she fixed a butterfly bandage across the cut on his cheek as she said, 'Come back in a week to have the sutures removed. Don't get them wet.'

She eased the boy to a sitting position. 'Dizzy?'

'Naw.'

'Then you can go.'

Lonnie maneuvered himself off the table, his movements slow and cautious.

She helped him put on what used to be a shirt. 'Where's your coat?'

'One of the guys has it. It was new and I didn't wanna ruin it.'

Too bad he didn't give his own hide the same consideration. 'Next time you play poker use toothpicks,' she suggested. 'It'll be less dangerous.'

Kirsten accompanied him to the door. Before he disappeared from view she said, 'Oh, and Lonnie? Let yourself heal before you get into another argument, OK?'

The boy grinned. 'Whatever you say, Doc.'

After that Kirsten and Jake saw myriad complaints, with little opportunity for conversation. By four o'clock the rush was over. Finding her private stock of canned soda depleted, she slipped into Irene's L-shaped office to raid the refrigerator and relax for a few minutes.

She rounded the corner to the sectioned-off portion which functioned as a mini-lounge and found Jake with his feet propped on top of the scarred coffee-table, sipping coffee from a golfer's mug.

'I gave Alfonso eighteen stitches,' he said. 'He didn't want them, of course. Apparently scars impress the girls, or so he believes.'

Kirsten grinned. 'How did you convince him?'

'I gave him a choice. He could either benefit from my sewing experience or I'd send him to the ER so a medical student could practice.'

'You didn't.'

'I did. Anyway, it worked. What about your patient?'

'Lonnie didn't argue about his stitches. But I beat you—he got twenty-five.'

'In the interest of peace, I hope Irene scheduled those two to come back at different times.'

From her desk around the corner the secretary-receptionist called over her shoulder, 'Never fear. I wasn't born yesterday.'

He addressed Kirsten. 'Does this happen often?'

Kirsten shrugged. 'Now and then.'

'You need a security guard.'

She sipped her drink. 'And what do I pay him with?'

'Maybe your landlord could provide one. After all, his property is at risk.'

Before Kirsten could explain about the building's owner an unfamiliar feminine voice, speaking in rapid-fire Spanish, captured her attention. Kirsten paused, struggling to pick out the few words in her bilingual vocabulary. Certain that a medical emergency had generated the commotion, she placed her soda can on the coffee-table and began to rise. Before she made it to her feet Irene stuck her head around the corner.

'Doctors, we have a very grateful mother. She'd like to talk to you.'

Kirsten went into the waiting-room, sensing Jake's presence behind her. The woman came up and hugged her, before she flung her arms around Jake.

'I am Alfonso's mother,' Mrs Rodriguez explained in broken English, her brown face wreathed in smiles. 'I must thank the doctors who helped my son.'

'It was nothing,' Kirsten protested. 'We were just doing our job.'

'No, no.' The woman shook her head. 'My son is good boy, but he has what you call temper. Anyway, I must repay you.'

Judging from the woman's clothing and her lack of a purse, it wouldn't be money. 'It isn't necessary.'

'Yes,' Mrs Rodriguez insisted. She bent over to pick up a brown paper sack from the floor. Glass banged on glass.

Realizing that they were about to receive a home-cooked gift, Kirsten hoped that it wasn't a jar of pickled pigs' feet. Another satisfied customer had given her the so-called culinary delight before Christmas and she hadn't had the stomach to try it. She didn't think she ever would.

Mrs Rodriguez pulled out two pint jars and pressed one into Kirsten's hands and one into Jake's.

Kirsten breathed a sigh of relief at the red contents. This she could handle.

'Strawberry jam,' Mrs Rodriguez announced with pride. 'Hope you like.'

'This is wonderful. Thank you.' She stole a glance at Jake. He eyed the gift as if a skull and crossbones, along with Mr Yuk—a happy face with its smile turned down and its tongue hanging out—were etched in the glass.

'I can't—' he began.

Insulted on her patient's behalf, Kirsten elbowed him to gain his attention. Pasting a smile on her face and gritting her teeth, she ordered in a voice barely above a whisper, 'You *will* take it.'

Jake's Adam's apple bobbed and his eyes rained fiery darts upon her. A second later he turned to Mrs Rodriguez. 'Thank you.'

'Good. I bring more when Alfonso come back.' The woman breezed outside, closing the door behind her with a quiet click.

The indignation Kirsten had suppressed bubbled to the surface. 'Your obligation to this clinic has just ended,' she said, her tone deadly quiet.

'What?'

'You heard me. I'm tired of the way you look down on my patients.'

'I do not.' He emphasized each word.

'That's the way it looks from my side. I don't need that kind of help.'

'Listen here—'

She dug her finger into his chest. '*You* listen. You're fired.'

CHAPTER FOUR

KIRSTEN'S words hung in the air, but she had no intention of calling them back. While Jake gaped at her she turned on her heel and marched past two equally astonished employees. Jake's true colors had finally come to light and she had witnesses.

And yet, as she stormed into her office, she knew that the subject wasn't closed. Jake wouldn't take his dismissal lightly. The heavy tread of footsteps and the door slamming behind her confirmed her instincts.

She pivoted to face him, noticing that his expression was one of controlled fury. 'If you're worried about your *obligation* consider yourself released.'

'If you want me to go I will. But first I plan to straighten out a few things.'

'There's nothing more to say.' She clamped her mouth into a hard line.

He advanced until he stood toe to toe with her. 'Oh, yes, there is. I don't know where or how you dreamed up the idea that I look down on your clients but you're wrong.'

'I saw the way you looked at those boys,' she accused. 'Admit it. You were disgusted with them.'

'It had nothing to do with the kids. I simply didn't want to land in the middle of unstable circumstances.'

'Huh.'

'To be honest, it reminded me of my ER days. Maybe you've forgotten the stabbings, the bar-room brawls and the shootings but I haven't.'

She rubbed her right temple. Most had been gruesome.

'We had a fight brewing one night, much like what you had here. One guy pulled a gun. Before anyone could do anything he fired. A wild bullet hit the orderly standing on my left.'

Her gaze landed on the scar above his eyebrow. Having been caught in the middle of a few altercations, she could well see the picture Jake had painted. However, she refused to concede anything to a man whose affluence colored his judgement. 'These boys didn't have a gun.'

'Are you positive? In case you've forgotten, there were eight teenagers in the room. That was a volatile situation, if I've ever seen one. You—*we*—were lucky your whistle defused it. Next time it may not.'

Kirsten recognized the truth in his statement, but she wouldn't acknowledge it now—not while she had Jake Marshall on trial. She brought up her second point.

'What about your reaction to Mrs Rodriguez's gift? It wasn't a bag of body parts, for heaven's sake, it was strawberry jam. *Everybody* likes jam.'

'I do, too.'

She placed both hands on her hips. 'Only the gourmet kind, right? Not home-made.'

'That has nothing to do with it.' A tic appeared in his jaw.

'Really.' She injected a disbelieving note into her voice. 'Then what does?'

'I'm allergic to strawberries.'

Kirsten's indignation deflated like a balloon that had come untied. She hadn't considered the possibility of a medical problem. 'Oh.'

'I was trying to explain my dilemma to Mrs Rodriguez when you dug your elbow into my stomach and commanded me to take her gift. I guess I should be grateful you didn't open a jar and force me into a taste test. It wouldn't have been a pretty sight.'

'I apologize.' Kirsten's tone was stiff. 'I didn't know. . .'

'If you weren't so quick to jump to conclusions, Doctor—at least where I'm concerned—we could have avoided all this.' His eyes narrowed. 'But I have a sneaking suspicion that these two incidents are only symptoms. Something else is on your mind.'

She stepped back. Anxious to put distance between them, she moved to her file cabinet—much like a boxer retreating to his corner. The clown smiled down at her. Without thinking, she reached upward to finger one of the red ruffles on its dress.

Jake was right: today's events in themselves meant nothing. Yet did she have the courage to voice her most damning piece of evidence?

'Does this have something to do with my absence last week?'

She seized the opening. Thrusting her hands into her pockets, she delivered her indictment in a quiet manner. 'You deserted sick people.'

He squared his jaw and narrowed his eyes. 'Desertion is a strong charge. One that I, and any other doctor, don't appreciate. I may be guilty of a lot of things, but neglect is *not* one of them.'

'Then what do you call making patients wait while you take the afternoon off to discuss financial matters?'

The puzzled lines around his eyes disappeared. 'I finally understand. If I'd been called away for a patient that would have been fine. But since it was my accountant. . .' His voice faded.

Kirsten remained silent.

'You, my dear Dr Holloway, are prejudiced.'

She folded her arms. 'That's not true. I have nothing against people in that profession. I do, however, object to professionals who place money before medicine.'

Jake moved closer. 'You're confusing me with someone else.'

Kirsten glanced at the clown, remembering its former owner and feeling a familiar ache in her heart. 'Am I?'

He nodded. 'I interviewed a man to handle my firm's finances, but we were finished by two o'clock. In the meantime, my colleague received word that his mother had had a stroke. I volunteered to cover while he flew to Dallas for a few days. Next thing I knew I had two emergency angioplasty cases.

'I couldn't come back because my assistant can't handle the procedure alone. You, on the other hand, didn't need me to diagnose bronchitis and strep throat.'

Kirsten felt suitably chastised.

'Contrary to what you might have thought, I wasn't sitting in front of the fireplace, sipping martinis.'

Her face warmed.

'I tried calling but the line was busy.'

That much was true. Their incoming phone line had buzzed all day. Each time she'd seen Irene the receptionist had had the phone cradled against her ear.

Jake leaned forward. 'Anything else on your mind?' 'N-no.'

'Fine. The next time something bothers you speak up before you imagine horrors that don't exist.'

'Next time?' she stammered. 'But—'

He clicked his fingers. 'Oh, yes, I've been fired. Why don't we meet at the Longhorn to discuss this?'

A tentative knock saved her. Kirsten skirted Jake to

open the door. Recognizing her small visitor, she said, 'Well, if it isn't Amanda.'

'Hi, Dr Holloway.' The child's upturned face revealed a toothless smile.

'Mandy,' her mother scolded from a distance, 'don't bother Dr Holloway.'

'It's OK,' Kirsten said, grateful for the momentary reprieve. She tugged on one of Amanda's flaxen braids. 'How was your allergy shot today?'

'Fine. I'm learning a new rhyme.'

'You are?'

Amanda nodded. 'But I can't tell you yet 'cause I don't have it all mem'rized.'

'Maybe next time,' Kirsten said.

'I'll tell you what part I do 'member.' Amanda's brown eyes sparkled with enthusiasm.

Kirsten glanced at Jake. Perhaps he'd tire of waiting and leave before she responded to his dinner invitation. Amy would consider her crazy but she didn't want to accept—it was too risky. If he shattered any more of her misconceptions she'd find him as attractive inside as out. She would *not* allow another physician who disagreed with her philosophy to tie her heart in knots. Once had been enough.

Jake lifted one eyebrow, folded his arms over his chest and leaned against her desk.

She addressed Amanda. 'Sure, go ahead.'

Amanda began her recitation. ' "Molly, my sister, and I fell out, and what do you think it was all about? I loved—" '

The youngster paused and wrinkled her face in concentration.

'Coffee,' Kirsten supplied.

' "Coffee and she loved—" ' Once again Amanda

paused. 'I don't 'member the rest yet.'

Tea, and that was the reason we couldn't agree.
Kirsten finished the poem in her mind, wishing Amanda
had chosen another rhyme. This one fitted her and Jake
to perfection. She stole a glance at him to see if he'd
caught the significance. His broad smile suggested that
he had.

'You almost have it,' Kirsten said.

'Yup.' Amanda crossed the threshold, tugging on the
string wrapped around her hand. A smiley-faced green
balloon cleared the frame and bobbed in the air above
her. ''Fore I go I'm s'posed to thank you for the pretty
b'loon. I've been wanting one just like it. I even wished
last night on a star.'

'I'm glad you got what you wanted.'

'Green's my fav'rite color,' she announced. 'I picked
it out of a box.'

'You made a good choice.'

'Come, Mandy. Let's go home.' Mrs Jenkins ushered
her daughter toward Irene's office.

Just then Amy strode past the doorway and Kirsten
stopped her. 'Who donated a box of balloons?'

Amy's face broke into a huge smile. 'Why, Dr
Marshall did. Along with a carton of drug samples.
Wasn't that nice?'

'Yeah.' *Jake? Balloons?* The two didn't seem to go
together. Surely Amy had made a mistake. Kirsten turned
to Jake, expecting a denial.

His mouth turned into a lazy smile. 'Shocked you,
didn't I?'

Kirsten blinked. 'I don't know what to say.'

'The usual response is "thank you". But you can
tell me that this evening. Seven o'clock. The Longhorn
Restaurant. Do you know where it is?'

Still dumbfounded, she could only nod.

'See you then.' Apparently satisfied with her response, or lack thereof, he left with a jaunty spring in his step.

Kirsten stared at his back, too surprised at the recent turn of events to protest.

Amy touched her arm. 'You OK? You look strange.' Her gaze turned knowing. 'Worried over what to wear?'

Kirsten pulled herself together and grabbed at Amy's excuse to avoid further explanations. 'Of course.' But, deep in her heart, she knew that clothes were the least of her problems where Jake Marshall was concerned.

Jake glanced at his watch. Kirsten wasn't due for another five minutes. He dug his hands into his overcoat, choosing to stand rather than sit on the wooden bench the steak restaurant had provided for waiting patrons.

The hostess approached on silent shoes. 'Your table is ready, sir.'

'I'll wait for my guest.'

'May we take your coat?'

'I'll keep it for now,' he told the young redhead. If Kirsten didn't appear by seven-fifteen he planned a quick exit.

Jake meandered across the foyer, aptly decorated in a western motif, and stood in front of a framed Terry Redlin print. The lights of the artist's historical town at night reminded him of the enlarged photograph in Kirsten's office depicting a lighted Ferris wheel.

He grinned, remembering the look of surprise on her face the moment she'd learned of his gift to the clinic. Her eyes had grown wide, making their contrasting pigments all the more obvious. He'd obviously ruined another of her stereotypical assumptions, and he couldn't wait to see what other misguided opinions resided in her head.

His reputation had grown over the years and he didn't concern himself with the occasional disgruntled individual. Those people were usually motivated by jealousy, and no amount of explanations or concessions on his part would ever change their minds.

Yet, with Kirsten, he *wanted* to break down the invisible barrier between them. He'd started this afternoon, but something else stood between them. Maybe she suffered from professional jealousy—he was expanding his private clinic while she struggled to keep her doors open—but he doubted it. His gut said that it was more serious and he'd learned to rely on his instincts.

One thing was certain—by the time their evening ended Jake would know her better than her own mother did. Provided she came.

The door swung open, delivering a blast of cold air. His pulse quickened with anticipation but settled into a steady rate as soon as a couple came into view. Thrusting his hands deep into his overcoat pockets, his fingers brushed against an old golf tee he'd found on the floor of his Jeep. Running his fingers along the chipped edge, he began to pace the floor.

His soles clicked against the wood and an occasional board creaked. Now he understood why hospitals muffled their waiting-rooms with wall-to-wall carpeting. He felt as jittery as the family members he encountered after performing one of his cardiac procedures.

Without losing a step, he checked his watch just as the hour changed. He'd always moved heaven and earth to accomplish whatever task he'd set before himself, and he didn't intend to stop now. Although his grandfather wouldn't point an accusing finger if Kirsten Holloway refused his services, Jake didn't want to see the unspoken disappointment in the old man's eyes.

Anxious for her to appear, Jake tensed. If Kirsten thought that, by staying away, the subject was closed she was in for a surprise. He wanted the situation resolved and he wanted it resolved to his satisfaction, even if it meant driving all over Kansas City to find her.

Failure was not in his vocabulary.

Kirsten tugged on the door and rushed inside the Longhorn Restaurant to escape the bitter cold. She'd heard of this place but its five-star rating had been enough to convince her that she couldn't afford the smallest bowl of soup. Jake Marshall might have a wallet to match his champagne taste but she didn't. Surely her finances could cover something to drink.

She paused in the foyer and waited for her eyes to adjust to the dim lighting. The delicious smells of char-broiled beef and baked potatoes made her stomach rumble. Wondering if she'd made the right decision, she fluffed her bangs and chewed on her bottom lip.

After Jake had left she'd debated her course of action with the ferocity of a ping-pong match. The idea of arriving at her answer by plucking the petals of a sunflower in the he-loves-me-he-loves-me-not routine became extremely appealing.

In the end the ridiculous box of balloons had forced her to rule in his favor. She'd never expected something so frivolous, so fanciful, from someone as driven as Jake Marshall. The cardiac drugs she could understand— those were readily available in his own office—but balloons? He had had to go out of his way to locate those. Maybe he did have a heart buried underneath his no-

nonsense exterior. And, if so, she was in danger of losing hers.

In the meantime, her patients could use his specialized medical skills while she took advantage of this once-in-a-lifetime opportunity to learn from a top-notch specialist. It didn't take a Nobel prize winner to see both the short- and long-term benefits he'd bring to her practise.

Rescinding his dismissal wouldn't take longer than the time it took to drink a mug of hot chocolate. She would have preferred to discuss their working relationship in the impersonal atmosphere of her office, but since it wasn't possible she'd get straight to business then be on her way before her heart softened any more than it already had.

Kirsten swallowed hard. It was easier to keep her emotions in line if she thought of him in terms of a cold-hearted, unfeeling, haughty specialist. She'd make certain that any future partners not only shared her vision but also possessed absolutely no sex appeal.

She took a fortifying breath and walked toward the hostess, wishing that her feet were headed in the opposite direction. 'Has Jakob Marshall arrived?'

The woman smiled. 'Yes, ma'am. He's waiting over there.'

Kirsten glanced in the direction indicated. Jake's set jaw and drawn eyebrows made him appear as forbidding as he had during their first encounter. The urge to leave before he saw her came on strongly, but in the same instant he turned his head.

He blinked as if he couldn't believe his eyes. Then the lines around his mouth and on his forehead relaxed and a satisfied grin spread over his face.

His apparent delight chased away her reluctance. It had been a long time since an eligible male had appeared excited to see her—at least not since the early days of her relationship with Edward Cox.

A burst of heat swept through her, making her glad that the dim lighting hid her heightened color. Certain that her smile wobbled as much as her legs, she focused on the hem of his wool coat. The knee-length garment flapped against his dark trousers with each long stride until he stood next to her.

In spite of the restaurant's inherent aroma, she detected the scent distinctive to Jake Marshall. Even if she lived to be a hundred the fragrance would conjure up vivid images of this man.

'I'm glad you came.'

'Did you think I wouldn't?'

'That was a possibility. Then again, some people tend to be fashionably late.' Jake moved behind her to help remove her parka.

His hands brushed across her back and she felt his warmth through her silk blouse. Every nerve ending jumped, and goose bumps of anticipation rose on her skin. She shivered. 'I'm afraid I'm not one of them.'

'Good, because I'm starved.' He handed her coat to the attendant, then shrugged off his own. Straightening his tie, he asked, 'Shall we?'

Conscious of her slightly rumpled clothing which, even after a laundering, didn't compare to the elegance of his casual wear, she nodded. For a fleeting moment she wished that time had permitted her to change into a fresh outfit, but it hadn't. Stifling a sigh, she followed the hostess to a table for two in a secluded corner.

'Enjoy your meal,' the woman told them.

Jake held out her chair. 'I hope you don't mind this spot. I'm always running into people I know so I chose a place where we could talk—and eat—in peace.'

'It's fine,' Kirsten stammered. Jake might consider this location only in terms of privacy but, to her, the burning votive candle in its clear glass cup and a long-stemmed red rosebud gave their isolation a romantic flavor.

For a brief second she fantasized that her handsome companion had planned this setting for an intimate purpose. The clink of silverware and a hearty laugh, coming from another table, broke into her thoughts. She had no business entertaining notions about what could never happen.

Chiding herself, Kirsten picked up the menu and focused on the choices. To her surprise, the prices weren't as exorbitant as she'd imagined. Perhaps she should enjoy the meal while she had the chance.

'I come here quite often. My personal favorite is the T-bone steak.'

She peered at him over the menu. 'Not the prime rib?'

His wide grin revealed his chipped tooth. 'Sorry to disappoint you.'

'Actually, I thought you'd be more interested in chicken or fish. Or don't you follow your own medical advice?'

'I do, but I also allow my patients to indulge themselves for special occasions.'

She placed the menu on the table, tracing the blocked embossed on the black vinyl cover. 'Is this a special occasion?'

'Actually, it's a celebration of sorts.'

Kirsten cleared her throat. 'Oh?'

Jake sipped from his water glass. 'That you're willing to be open-minded. At least where I'm concerned.'

She leaned back. 'I am? What makes you so sure?'

'You're here, aren't you?'

'I didn't have an opportunity to refuse.'

He waved aside her comment. 'You could have called and canceled.'

'I thought about it.'

'Why didn't you?'

Using an index finger, she drew circles in the moisture on the outside of the water goblet. 'I'm getting the impression that you wish I had.'

'No. I'm just trying to understand how my colleague's mind operates.'

'Refreshing your psychiatric skills, Dr Marshall?' she asked lightly.

'It never hurts to dust them off.'

Stalling for time, she shook out the elaborately folded napkin and placed it on her lap. 'It seemed sort of. . .' She hesitated, searching for the right descriptive word.

'Spineless?' Jake supplied.

She smiled. 'Yes.'

'I know people who, given the same circumstances, wouldn't have bothered to show up or call.'

'So do I, but I'm not like "most people".'

Jake met her gaze. 'No, you're not,' he said quietly.

His tone gave nothing away, leaving her without a clue as to whether he thought her differences were good or bad. She debated making a flippant comment to defuse the charged moment, then decided against it. For some undefinable reason she didn't want to know if he considered her odd.

Uncertainty washed over her. She looked down and adjusted the napkin on her lap.

'Do you know why I think you came?'

Unsure of the reasons herself, she couldn't restrain her curiosity. 'No, but I'm certain you'll tell me.'

'You realized I wasn't such a bad guy after all.'

The perfect opportunity to tell him that he was correct—that she'd fired him in haste, that she wanted him back—stared her in the face. But somehow she knew that once she'd admitted her error she'd have no reason to prolong the evening. And she wanted to linger as much as she wanted to keep Diana's clinic open. For the next hour she wanted to live the fantasy of being a handsome man's dinner guest.

'Sure of yourself, aren't you?'

'Yes.'

'Let's just say I haven't made my final diagnosis. I'm waiting for a second opinion.' She paused. 'What if I hadn't come?'

'I'd have found you,' he said without equivocation.

The waiter approached and Kirsten accepted his interruption with relief. After giving their orders, Jake said, 'By the way, my assistant sends his regards. I believe he knew you in med school. Scott Rydell.'

Picturing the doctor in question, she smiled. 'Scott was—is—brilliant.'

'He says the same thing about you.'

She waved aside the comment. 'I studied hard.'

'According to him, you had a number of job offers.'

Remembering the practices who had vied for her commitment, she smiled. Downplaying her marketability, she said, 'A few.'

'What made you choose the family health center over another group?'

'You mean some place more profitable or lucrative? With most evenings free and working one weekend a month?'

He shrugged. 'After scrimping through years of medical training most doctors are ready to earn a comfortable income and pay off their debts. I know I was.'

'You?'

'Don't look so shocked. I may be the fourth generation of physicians in the Marshall family but my grandfather insisted that I struggle through like everyone else. Living on a shoestring was supposed to build my character.'

'Did it?' she teased.

'You tell me. In any event, you didn't answer my question.'

She shrugged. 'Diana needed me.'

'What did your parents say about your decision?'

'My mother understood my reasons and wasn't surprised by my choice. My father died while I was in college. Besides, Diana's clinic is listed as an underserved area. After working for three years my loan will be forgiven.'

'And now that she's gone?'

'As long as the center's doors remain open I'll be OK. If not, I'll have to relocate.'

Jake's eyes became intent. 'Is there a chance that you'll have to close your facility?'

'Anything's possible,' she replied in a light-hearted tone. If she didn't come up with some financial backing the possibility grew stronger with each passing week. That, however, was her problem and not his.

Wanting to direct his attention elsewhere, she asked, 'What do you do in your spare time?'

'My whole family plays golf. Even my grandmother. My grandfather taught us when we were kids, just like his dad taught him.' Jake smiled. 'Of course he claims there are no courses like the ones in his beloved Scotland.'

Just then their food arrived, and Kirsten waited until they were alone before asking her next question. 'I've heard of your grandfather, but I don't recall any mention of your dad.'

Jake peppered his baked potato. 'You wouldn't. He died from hepatitis when I was seven. Apparently he contracted it from one of his patients—rather unfortunate, for a surgeon. My mother had rheumatic fever as a child and, since her heart was never strong, she passed away when my brother was born.'

Kirsten empathized with him. Tragedy gave them a common bond, just as it had drawn her and her closest friends together. 'Then you spent a lot of time with your grandparents?'

His teeth gleamed in the candlelight. 'My granddad credits my brother and me for his white hair.'

'Is your brother in medicine too?'

Jake shook his head. 'He's a computer whiz. Works for a software company.'

'And now you're responsible for the Marshall Clinic.'

'More or less. Even though Ian, my grandfather, has retired he likes to monitor our progress. He did an excellent job of building up the practice but for years he preferred a family-oriented business. It took some time and a lot of convincing, but he finally recognized the need to round out his services by adding specialists.

'Luckily,' Jake continued, cutting into his steak, 'he's an excellent judge of character and skill. Everyone he's brought on board has become well known in their field.'

'Including his grandson.'

Jake grinned. 'I'm glad you think so.'

Kirsten savored the taste of well-seasoned beef cooked to perfection. 'And now you're expanding again.'

Jake nodded. 'Everyone wants the best medical care, which puts a strain on the physicians—not to mention wear and tear on the equipment. To keep up with the demand we have to add more staff, and to do that we need more office space.'

'A vicious circle.'

'I'm afraid so.'

But when does it end? she wanted to ask. Instead, she changed the subject. 'Is there a fifth generation of Marshalls to take over someday?'

'My brother is handling that. I have two nieces and one nephew.'

She wiped her mouth. 'You aren't interested in helping him?' she asked lightly. 'Surely some woman has tried to obtain the coveted position of Mrs Jake Marshall.'

'I came close once.' He paused, as if deep in his memory. When he spoke again his tone possessed a far-off quality. 'She didn't want to raise a family alone and since I was gone most of the time. . .' His voice faded.

'I'm sorry,' Kirsten murmured.

'What about you?' he asked.

She scooted a bite-sized piece of steak around her plate. 'I came close, too. But I soon realized that Edward and I wanted different things. He wanted the fame and fortune associated with being a doctor and I wasn't interested in profiting from people's misery.'

'So all physicians should be penniless and receive jars of strawberry jam as payment for services rendered?' His smile was lopsided with amusement as he shook his head. 'You were born in the wrong century, my dear. You should have practiced medicine a hundred years ago when bartering and payment with fresh vegetables were common.'

'We should earn a decent living,' she corrected, 'not be greedy.'

'Ah, but what's "decent"? Everyone's standards vary.'

'Yes, but some are more interested in their bank statements and expensive hobbies than their patients.'

The smile on his face disappeared. 'And how have you categorized me?'

CHAPTER FIVE

STALLING for time, Kirsten raised the heavy mug of hot chocolate to her mouth. If she'd been asked the same question a few days or even a few hours ago—how she had characterized Jake—she would have answered without any hesitation. Now, however, she couldn't.

Sipping the lukewarm liquid, she glanced at him. His eyes were intent, his expression stoic, his shoulders squared. Every part of him appeared as if he expected bad news and had braced himself for it.

Insight flashed with a laser-like intensity. Jake knew what she thought of him—she hadn't held anything back during their discussion in her office. No, he wanted to discover if she had changed her opinion.

She lowered the cup but kept her hands wrapped around it for warmth. Studying Jake while summoning courage to admit the truth, she licked her lips and tasted the sweetness of marshmallow foam.

Jake's gaze moved to her mouth, his countenance revealing a hunger totally unrelated to food. Empowered by his obvious interest, her lips tingled and her hands itched to caress his clean-shaven face, the slightly raised scar on his forehead, his hard biceps and his broad shoulders.

How she wished they were alone, totally alone, but regretfully they weren't. If the time and place had been appropriate she would have welcomed his kiss and his embrace, drinking in his male scent as if she couldn't survive without it.

With effort, she pushed aside the notion. She didn't have time for a romantic interlude. The price of a short-term affair was too costly in terms of the energy it would require. Just as a toddler needed supervision to steer him from unseen dangers and pitfalls, the health center demanded every ounce of her attention until it reached solid financial footing. She couldn't afford to lose the little ground she had gained.

Trying to lighten the mood and set her thoughts on something less heady, she tapped an index finger against her right temple. 'Let's see. Greedy or decent?' Screwing her face up theatrically and looking upwards at the ceiling as if consulting her Maker, she added, 'If I say decent it will go to his head.'

Out of the corner of one eye she watched a slow grin spread over his face.

'Since he donated enough balloons to last for the next ten years I can't label him greedy either.' Kirsten threw up her hands and turned her full attention on Jake. Smiling, she said, 'I guess you're somewhere in between.'

'Spoken like a true diplomat.'

'Just send me on the next peace-keeping mission. I can't go without my whistle, though.'

He laughed. The sound of his mirth did strange things to her heart, creating a wish to hear it on a regular basis.

The waiter discreetly arrived to remove the dirty dishes. After declining a refill of hot chocolate, she pointed to Jake's face. 'You never said, but were you injured when you had the skirmish in ER?'

Jake ran two fingers over the thin line above his eyebrow. 'Nothing so noble, I'm afraid. My brother and I were practicing our golf swings. I was about fifteen and he had just gotten a set of clubs for his thirteenth birthday. Being the expert that I was, I stood by to give him a few pointers.'

Kirsten winced with sympathy, picturing what had happened. 'Ouch.'

'Actually, he didn't hit me. Don't ask me how, but he knocked my grandmother's cuckoo clock off the wall. A piece of the fancy scrollwork caught me as it landed.'

'You were lucky it missed your eye.'

'No kidding. Anyway, blood spattered everywhere, or so it seemed. Keith dropped his iron to find a towel. I had my hands covering my face so I didn't notice his club on the floor. I tripped, fell and chipped my tooth on the table leg.'

Kirsten's jaw dropped at his story and she covered her mouth with one hand. 'What did your grandparents say?'

'Not much. They knew Keith and I suffered both mental and physical anguish for ignoring Grams's rules. We never practiced anything but putting inside the house again.'

'No punishment for breaking her clock?'

Jake nodded. 'Keith had to replace it which was tough, considering they'd bought it in Germany on their fortieth wedding anniversary.'

'You got off scot-free?'

'Afraid not,' he said, sounding rueful. 'I had to give up my key to the golf cart for a month.'

'What a horrible fate,' she teased.

'Hey, at the time it was.' He sounded indignant. 'Not only did I have to suffer through stitches but I had to carry my own bag of clubs. It's degrading for a teenager to lose his wheels.'

Kirsten made a point of studying his shoulders. They were wide and solid and perfect. 'Looks like you didn't suffer any long-term after-effects.'

Jake grinned. 'The benefits outweighed the pain.'

She could well imagine those benefits—a good tan, strong muscles, a trim body from the extra walking, not to mention the female attention he'd no doubt received because of his injury.

'Your grandparents are to be commended for teaching responsibility.'

'It wasn't easy. But now that you know I'm dependable and trustworthy, is this the time to ask if I can have my job back?' His eyes sparkled with delight, as if he already knew her answer.

Deciding to keep him in suspense a little longer, she used an offhanded tone. 'Should I let you?'

'Of course.'

'Give me one good reason.'

'I can give you several. One, you still need another physician. Two, after tonight I'm not a stranger any more. Three. . .' he dug in his pants pocket, pulled out a shiny piece of metal and held it aloft like a talisman '. . .I still have the clinic's key.'

'Locks can be changed,' she reminded him.

Lowering his hand, he shook his head. 'Too costly. It would be cheaper to keep me on staff.'

'Do you really *want* to come back?' Before he could answer she continued, 'You originally offered your services out of an obligation. As I recall, when I first met you, you didn't seem too excited over the prospect. I'd have thought you'd be happy to be released from those ties.'

With his lips pursed and his brow furrowed into a line, he toyed with the key. Finally, he answered, 'I suppose I should be. To be honest, I didn't want to spend my days there.'

'What made you change your mind?'

Jake rubbed his chin with one palm. 'My schedule at the clinic seems to be working, in spite of my dire predictions. But it wasn't until you gave me an easy way out that I realized I would have failed—that somehow I'd be cheating in the grand scheme of things.' He shrugged. 'My decision probably doesn't make sense to you—not while my own matters are hanging upside down—but. . .'

She nodded, assigning extra points in his favor on her mental scoreboard. 'Believe it or not, it does.'

Studying his capable hands, the silver-plated key held in his fingertips represented hope. With Jake's help and her hard work she could set her dreams on a more firm foundation than they were at present.

Kirsten's gaze rested on his features. Although she'd wanted to avoid this evening, now she was glad she hadn't.

The corners of his mouth twitched. 'I have one final argument. If I have to document on my curriculum vitae that I was fired after two weeks I'll become depressed, turn to alcohol and wild women, lose my career, live in a cardboard box under some bridge and never be seen again.'

His expression of abject misery brought a smile to her face. 'Such melodrama.' Scooting her chair back, she held out her hand and rose.

After a few seconds of hesitation Jake dropped the key into her palm.

Kirsten hefted the object. 'You've been quite convincing this evening, Dr Marshall. Just for the record, the wining and dining wasn't necessary. I'd made up my mind before I walked through the door.'

He raised one eyebrow.

She tossed the key toward him.

He caught it in mid-air. In the next instant his frozen features relaxed. 'Does this mean what I think it means?'

She nodded. 'Don't lose it.'

'I won't. I promise. See you Thursday.'

Her pulse rate jumped at the prospect of seeing him again so soon, but she quickly rationalized her reaction. The idea of having time to recruit a physician's assistant, search out supporters and catch up on her paperwork caused her excitement. It had absolutely nothing to do with seeing him again.

But, in her heart, she knew she was fooling herself.

'Short of keeping Tommy inside the house all day, I don't know what to do. He's always getting hurt.' Julie Reed's shoulders were slumped. Even though exhaustion lined her face and she spoke with exasperation, she looked fondly on her son.

It was Thursday morning and Kirsten enjoyed the slower pace that Jake's presence had made possible. She dabbed at the bleeding gash on the four-year-old's shin and prepared to suture the torn edges together. 'He does seem accident-prone,' she said, noticing the black and blue discolorations along the boy's leg.

'You don't suppose he has something like,' Julie leaned forward and lowered her voice to a whisper, 'a brain tumor, do you?' Her chin quivered and worry shone out of both brown eyes.

Not wanting to belittle the mother's anxiety, Kirsten allowed a small smile. 'Has he had any headaches or nausea?'

'No. He eats constantly.'

Considering the boy's stocky frame and above-average height, Kirsten believed it. 'Has he been lethargic, had any personality changes or seemed to forget things he's known or learned?'

Julie shook his head. 'He catches on real quick.'

'Then I'd rule out an intracranial mass. Bumps and bruises, gashes and broken arms aren't uncommon in over-active children.'

Julie sighed. 'I know. It seems worse because we've had to bring him in for one thing or another every month for the last five.'

'Exploring is part of learning and growing older,' Kirsten advised. 'Just be patient.'

Although Kirsten didn't mention the subject of abuse she always kept on the alert. A physician couldn't afford to overlook the possibility whenever youngsters suffered frequent injuries. While her instincts didn't signal any warning in this particular case it wouldn't hurt to keep an eagle eye on the boy.

Nor would it hurt to restudy the medical records sent by Tommy's former physician in case she'd overlooked a pattern.

'I know.' The dishwater-blonde woman sighed, clutching Tommy's small arm with work-reddened hands. 'He's simply clumsy. I've never seen anyone fall over things, including his own feet, so much. That's what happened this time, too.'

'He tripped?'

Julie nodded. 'He never looks where he's going. I was scrubbing the floor and he fell over the mop bucket.'

'I didn't mean to, Mom,' Tommy said.

'I know, hon.' Julie's tired voice reflected resignation. 'I just wish you'd watch where you're going.'

'I will,' he promised, his dark eyes wide and his expression solemn.

'At least until next time,' Julie said.

The boy grinned.

As Kirsten tied the last knot she praised his fortitude. Contrary to other children she treated, Tommy bore the sharp sting of needles and anesthetic in stoic silence.

'I want him back in about a week to have the stitches removed. Don't get them dirty or wet,' she instructed. Stripping off her gloves while Julie helped her son to sit up, she added, 'Be careful where you walk so you don't bump your leg. We don't want to sew you up again.'

'OK,' Tommy said.

'I'll make certain,' Julie broke in, 'even if I have to sit on him.'

He giggled. 'You can't sit on me. You'll squash me.'

Julie tousled the light hair so similar to her own and smiled. 'True.'

Privately, Kirsten wondered how the slender mother could crush anything, much less her solidly built son. The woman barely topped five feet and couldn't weigh more than a hundred pounds.

Julie helped the boy to zip his jeans while Kirsten washed her hands.

'I'll give him a quick once-over before you go. Just to make certain he didn't hurt anything else,' she added tactfully.

Kirsten crouched down to Tommy's eye level and lifted up his shirt to listen to his chest. Thankfully she saw no bruises, felt nothing out of the ordinary. 'Do you go to pre-school?'

He shook his head. 'Jus' story hour at the li-berry.'

'Do you like the friends there?'

'Yeah. We do fun things. But I don' like to color.'

'Why not?'

''Cause I can't stay in the lines. They're fuzzy, like my teddy bear.'

The two women stared at each other. Moving to the corner of the room where they kept a box of toys, Kirsten selected a coloring book which featured two children with an umbrella. She held it aloft. 'Can you tell me what this book is about?'

Tommy's eyes narrowed until they became small slits. 'Animals. In a barn.'

'Are you sure?' Kirsten watched his reaction.

He squinted again before he nodded. 'Uh-huh.'

Kirsten glanced at Julie who stared at her son with amazement. 'I'd recommend an eye appointment,' she said softly. 'The sooner the better.'

Julie nodded, her shoulders slumped underneath the oversized flannel shirt which had worn thin from repeated washing. 'Will he need glasses?'

'Probably,' Kirsten answered. 'There is a Vision USA program which provides free eye care to families who qualify.'

Julie's face brightened and Kirsten knew she had identified another concern. 'Really?'

'The American Optometric Association has nearly eight thousand members who volunteer their services for needy children and adults. They focus on low-income households.'

'What do we do?'

'You have to meet certain conditions to receive a comprehensive optometrist's exam. One person in the household has to have a job, no health insurance and meet their income guidelines. If you'd like, Irene can give you the application forms on your way out. There's a toll-free number, too.'

Julie looked down on her son and fingered his locks. 'Will it pay for his glasses?'

'I can't say for sure. I only know that it covers

the examination. Even so, every little bit helps.'

'You're right.'

'If you find that you don't meet their criteria, for whatever reason, then call me and I'll see if I can arrange something else. OK?'

Julie nodded. 'Thanks, Dr Holloway.'

Kirsten playfully tugged Tommy's ear lobe. 'Be good until next week, squirt.' Having potentially solved Tommy's problems, she strode out of the room with her spirits soaring.

Seeing the figure waiting in the hallway, she stopped in her tracks and her good mood evaporated. The brown-haired, hawk-faced, dressed-for-success landlord, Robert Carlton, never came around unless he brought bad news. His whole character reeked like his cheap cologne.

Forcing her mouth into a small curve, she called out half-hearted greetings.

'Dr Holloway,' he acknowledged. His smile bared his teeth but didn't reflect itself in his eyes. 'May I have a moment of your time?'

Kirsten clenched her jaw at the sound of a voice as oily as his slicked-back hair. 'Of course. Let's go into my office.'

Out of the corner of one eye she saw Jake come out of room two, his interest in her visitor unmistakable. Anxious to discover Carlton's purpose and send him on his way as quickly as possible, she ushered him into her private area and closed the door.

'I'm sorry to tell you I have to raise the rent,' he said without any trace of apology in his voice as he settled into the chair across from her desk. 'Nothing personal, you understand.'

Pride wouldn't allow her to reveal her deep dismay. She steeled her face and raised one eyebrow. 'Again?'

He inspected his large ruby ring. 'With tax increases and the high cost of maintenance, I really have no choice.'

'Maintenance?' She was incredulous that he dared to label his stop-gap measures with such a word. She and her staff, including Irene's husband, patched as much as they could themselves because Carlton had a tendency to raise the rent whenever he replaced something.

'If I remember correctly, I re-plumbed the bathroom a few months ago.'

'Only because you didn't provide any heat to keep the water-pipes from freezing.'

He went on. 'As a show of my good faith, the increase won't go into effect until next month.'

Two weeks. How generous, she thought, gritting her teeth. 'Then you're planning to make the repairs I suggested in my last letter?'

'In due time, Dr Holloway. In due time.'

Which translated in Kirsten's mind as not anytime soon, if ever.

'By the way, I caught a glimpse of the fellow you have working here. A new partner?' he asked smoothly.

'Just someone filling in.'

'Temporarily or on a regular basis?'

Sensing that she was about to fall into a well-laid trap, she weighed her answer. 'Dr Marshall's time with us is temporary.'

'I see.' Carlton met her gaze. 'I'm glad to hear it. If he were permanent, why, that would shed new light on our business arrangement.'

Kirsten narrowed her eyes. 'Oh?'

Carlton nodded. 'Two physicians equals twice as many patients. That translates into twice as much wear and tear on my building.'

'Which also means twice as much rent?' she asked, unable to keep the sarcasm out of her voice in spite of her vow to not antagonize this man.

He crossed his legs, the crease in his black trousers crisp. 'Oh, no. A fifty-per-cent increase comes to mind, although I could be persuaded to negotiate a more mutually beneficial arrangement.' He wiggled his shaggy eyebrows.

Suppressing a shiver of distaste, she knew what he meant by 'mutually beneficial'. Although she was committed to the people in this neighborhood, she couldn't agree to his terms and still live with herself. Hiding her hands in her lap, Kirsten clenched her fists.

He waved one hand, the red stone of his ring flashing. 'In any event, we can discuss those small details after you actually hire someone.'

Filled with indignation, she clutched a pencil to keep her hands from trembling. 'I've been going through Diana's past records, you know. You've raised the rent quite often since she was killed.'

Carlton rose to his feet, his lips twisted into a half-smile. 'It is unfortunate, but my understanding with Diana ended with her death.'

He rounded the corner of her desk and clapped a hand on her shoulder. His proximity brought another wave of his nauseating scent to her nostrils. 'If you want the breaks I gave her then we have to make our own agreement.'

Kirsten tensed, his action making her feel cheap and dirty. 'Thanks, but I'll manage.'

Apparently unconcerned by her obvious dislike, Carlton shrugged and released her to reach inside the inner pocket of his suit coat. He pulled an embossed business card out and propped it against the telephone.

'If you change your mind here's my number. In the meantime, your payment is due on the fifteenth. Have a nice day.'

The moment he left she stripped off the white jacket, soiled by Carlton's touch, and replaced it with a fresh one. Next she flung open a window, anxious to clear the air of Carlton's odor. Oh, Diana, she cried out inside. What did you do?

Kirsten had always dismissed Carlton's leers and innuendos, but she'd never realized that Diana had fallen victim to the man's sleazy tactics. Her friend had obviously decided that desperate circumstances required desperate measures, and the realization saddened her.

Feeling the need for a change of scenery, she rushed from the room and ran into Jake outside the lounge.

Grabbing her by the shoulders, he steadied her. 'Where's the Code Blue?' His eyes narrowed as he studied her face. He placed his palm on her forehead. 'Are you OK?'

For an odd moment she wanted to snuggle into his hand, like a tiny kitten enjoying a loving caress. 'I'm fine. Why do you ask?'

'You're as white as your lab coat.'

'Fluorescent lights tend to wash out one's complexion.'

'In a few minutes?' He raised one eyebrow in disbelief. 'I saw the fellow who came in. If he's a prospective employee I'd say he doesn't have a chance.'

'That was our landlord. Robert Carlton.'

'Paying a social call, perhaps?' Jake's eyes were intent.

She avoided his gaze. 'No. Business.' Rubbing the back of her neck, she cleared her throat. 'Anyway, I need something to drink.'

He stepped aside.

When she returned with a large tumbler of ice water she found Jake lounging against the wall where she had left him.

'Feeling better?' he asked.

She saluted him with the cup and began walking toward her office. 'Great.'

Jake matched her strides. 'So, what happened with the landlord?'

'He raised the rent.'

'How much?'

'Any amount is too much. On the other hand, he's willing to strike a bargain.'

Something in her tone must have alerted him because Jake grabbed her elbow and brought her to a sudden halt. His eyes turned the color of flint and his mouth became a hard line. 'What kind of bargain?'

'One that I won't consider so don't worry.' She noticed how Jake's hand didn't evoke the same response that Carlton's had. 'If I get a permanent partner he'll raise my rent again.'

'Why?'

'Double wear and tear on his property. Or so he claims.'

'That's ridiculous. I'd like to tell him exactly—'

She touched his forearm. 'I'll start looking for another building. In the meantime, I can't antagonize him.'

He fell silent. 'Can you afford the increase?'

'I don't know,' she answered honestly. Taking a breath, she called up a smile. 'One way or another, we'll manage. We have so far.'

'Such optimism.'

'Of course. Life is more tolerable if one describes

a glass as half-full rather than half-empty. Wouldn't you agree?'

'If there's anything I can do to get Carlton off your back, let me know.'

Her insides twisted at the literal picture of Jake's comment. Carlton's hand on her person had been bad enough—she couldn't imagine anything worse. Hiding behind levity, she asked, 'Know anyone who has a vacant building in this neighborhood?'

Jake shook his head. 'Sorry.'

Kirsten stepped inside her office and set her drink on the desk as she sniffed the air. All traces of Carlton's presence had disappeared, making her feel safe in lowering the window.

Jake's voice came from behind her. 'What are you trying to do in here? Freeze to death? Even your doll is turning blue.'

She grinned at his silly remark. 'The room seemed stuffy.'

He looked as if he didn't believe her but didn't press the issue. 'I meant to ask something earlier, but I forgot until now. I reviewed your referral list and noticed the names of several top-notch physicians missing.'

'Oh, really? Which ones?'

'Dr Gordon, the urologist. I believe I referred one of your patients to him a week ago.'

Kirsten sat behind her desk. 'Irene talked to me about it. I sent him to Dr Appleby instead.'

'Why? What's wrong with Harold Gordon?'

She picked up Carlton's business card with two fingers and threw it in the trash can. 'He's a fine doctor—'

'Then why didn't you—?'

'—but Dr Gordon won't see my patients.'

Jake blinked. 'He won't?'

Her hair bounced as she shook her head. 'Supposedly, one of my referrals for a vasectomy had a lice infestation.'

'Did he?'

'I've seen this fellow many times, both before and after his consultation. I've never found any indications of lice. Anyway, because of that incident I now send my cases to several other urologists, who are equally good.'

'I see.' He paused, apparently mulling over the information. 'Most of the specialists on your list are well known so I'm surprised you don't have Sam Bailey down for surgical consultations.'

At the sound of the familiar name Kirsten froze. 'I'm satisfied with the ones I use.'

'Sam is a great guy and an excellent surgeon. I'm sure he'd be happy to help out. We golf together so I know him well. If you'd like, I could talk to him—'

Her 'No' came out more forcefully than she'd intended. Softening her tone, she kept her gaze focused on the upper left pocket of his lab coat which was embroidered with his name in red script. 'Thanks, anyway.'

Jake leaned one hip against her desk. 'There's more to this than you're telling me. I'm not leaving until I find out.'

Let it drop, Jake, she silently begged. She stood up and moved across the room to rifle through her file cabinet for a folder. 'I've made arrangements with the doctors on my list. I'm happy with their services and I'm not looking to replace them. That's all it is.'

He folded his arms high up on his chest. 'Give me one good reason why I can't ask a surgeon of his caliber to accept some of your referrals.'

She sat down again. 'Because I'm the boss. I have the final authority. Remember?'

'That's a cop-out. Give me another.'

Kirsten rubbed her temples. After dealing with Carlton, she didn't have enough emotional energy to dredge up the past.

'You know he's considered the best.'

'I've heard of his reputation.'

'You sound as if you don't agree.'

She raised her eyebrows.

'Ah, I get it.' His eyes glimmered with understanding. 'He gave you a rough time during med school, I'll bet. He's known for that. You shouldn't take it personally.'

Jake's final words grated like fingernails on a chalkboard.

'I take what he did very personally,' she said in a deadly calm voice, 'even though it had nothing to do with my training.' Seeing Jake's puzzled expression, she stated the facts as she saw them—the same facts she'd lived with for the past seventeen years.

'Dr Bailey killed my sister.'

CHAPTER SIX

JAKE'S jaw went slack and his eyes widened. 'When?'

Kirsten braced herself for a barrage of questions. 'I was twelve. Darcy was nine.' Her voice sharpened. 'Before you tell me that I was too young to understand all the details—don't. Once I entered my training a friend who worked in Medical Records found the chart for me.'

Kirsten would be for ever grateful to Ellen for helping her learn the truth, even though it had been painful. Ellen's death, a short time ago, had hit her as hard as Darcy's. Then again, it wasn't surprising. Kirsten and her three buddies—Bethany Trahern Lockwood, Ellen McGraw and Naomi Stewart—had been as close as sisters during their teenage and college years.

'What happened?'

She remembered those days well—her sister's fever, her pain, not to mention the hours at the hospital waiting for help, believing that the surgeon's wait-and-see attitude had been prudent. Instead of relaying all that information, she gave a condensed version. 'Darcy had appendicitis. Dr Bailey chose not to operate. It burst and she died from peritonitis.'

Jake's brow furrowed. 'Sometimes the diagnosis is hard to make.'

'I agree. But even after the surgical resident wanted to intervene our illustrious surgeon vetoed the idea. Mom overheard him saying that he didn't want to tie up the only empty operating room in case a *paying* customer came in. Darcy could wait.'

He shook his head. 'That doesn't sound like the Sam Bailey I know.'

'My mother didn't think he was joking.' Softening her tone, she mused aloud, 'Maybe if my parents had found the money to see someone else. . . Maybe if we'd had a family physician to watch out for Darcy and keep tabs on Bailey. . .' She sighed. 'Unfortunately, we'll never know.'

He crossed his arms. 'Didn't the hospital conduct an investigation?'

'I didn't have access to that information so I really can't say.'

'If it was a case of malpractice. . .'

'Do you doubt me?'

He winced. 'No, but you know that physicians base their decisions on experience. Sometimes the treatment initiated is a judgement call.'

'You're free to believe whatever you want,' she replied, stiffly. 'I, however, spent considerable time studying her chart.'

'If you felt so strongly why didn't you come forward?'

'What good would it have done? By that time the case was nearly fifteen years old. My sister and father were gone and my mother didn't want to dredge up the past.'

'The question is—did you?'

Kirsten didn't hesitate. 'Yes. I pictured the reputable Dr Bailey on the witness stand, with all the incriminating evidence brought before a jury. He'd break down, admit he'd made a gross error and beg our forgiveness.'

'And now?'

It had taken a long time—years, in fact—but with the help of Naomi, Beth and Ellen as her private support group she'd come to terms with the situation. She glanced at the clown. 'I'd rather spend my energy and financial resources on the living.'

'That's a healthy remark. It's good to accept the things you can't change.'

'Thanks, Dr Freud,' she said, wryly. 'So, if you're worried that I'll take out a full-page ad in the *Kansas City Star* against Sam Bailey, you can rest easy.'

He pantomimed his relief by wiping his brow. 'Thank God.'

'It doesn't mean, however, that I intend to let him touch my patients,' she warned. 'I refuse to refer anyone to a physician who's more concerned with money than with medical care.'

She reached out to grab his hand. 'Do you also see why this clinic is so important to me? I want to plug the holes that working-class poor people fall into through no fault of their own. I have to prevent another tragedy like the one with my sister.'

'I understand your motives,' he said thoughtfully. 'But with your finances stretched so thin. . .' His voice died.

'I know.' She sighed, releasing his fingers. 'The possibility of closing this center hangs over my head like the sword of Damocles but, to me, it isn't an option.'

'Why not? There are other practices—'

'Where the office staff hound my people to pay bills they can't afford?' She shook her head. 'No way. They either won't come or they'll wait until their conditions are so far advanced that they're beyond help.'

'You may not have a choice,' he reminded her.

'There are always choices. Maybe not the ones I'd like, but they still exist.' Kirsten pointed to the clown. 'Darcy won that doll at a fair and it became her prized possession. Now, whenever I see Emmaline I'm reminded of my little sister. For Darcy's sake and for other children like her, I can't give up.'

A few hours later Jake flipped through the documents inside Chester Olsen's folder. 'I see your blood pressure is normal.'

Seated on the examination table with his legs dangling over the side, the seventy-year-old man nodded his balding head. 'After I went to the public library and read about hypertension—learning isn't just for you young whippersnappers; I taught school for forty years, you know—I decided to follow Dr Holloway's instructions to the letter.'

'So you're watching your salt intake?'

'Most definitely.'

'Taking your medication?'

'Religiously.'

'Exercising?'

'Faithfully. The senior citizen bus takes me to one of the malls almost every day. There's usually someone who wants to shop so I just get off wherever the driver stops.' Chester leaned closer. 'It's amazing how the women, even at my age, insist on going to the stores. You suppose it's an addiction, like alcohol or cigarettes?'

Jake grinned. 'Trying to trap me, aren't you?'

Chester guffawed. 'Expect so. Anyway, my Marie loved to browse. Didn't buy anything, but she insisted on looking. I teased her a lot over her little habit.'

Concentrating on the man's heart sounds, Jake paid scant attention to Chester's ramblings.

'I could go to the Senior Center but, with my Marie gone now, being in the mall reminds me of her.' He continued in a reminiscent tone. 'We always stopped for an Orange Julius drink before we came home.'

'I don't believe I've ever had one.' Jake moved to check Chester's ankles for swelling.

'You must try one. They're delicious.'

Jake couldn't help but notice the bottoms of Chester's trousers. Although he had obviously worn his best clothes—a pair of brown dress trousers and a beige shirt—staples, spaced at even intervals, held the hem in place.

For a fleeting moment Jake wondered if he'd be like this elderly gentleman in twenty-five or thirty years— wandering the halls of the Marshall Clinic for exercise, staples holding his clothes together, alone. While Chester had memories of his wife to hold dear, all Jake would have were the memories of his work and the countless patients who eventually ran together in his mind.

The prospect was grim.

Jake cleared his throat. 'Looks like you're in fine shape, Mr Olsen.'

Chester buttoned his shirt. 'So you'll give me my pills?'

'Amy will bring in another supply of diuretics. Don't forget to come back in a month so she can check your blood pressure.'

With his foot, Jake located the pedal to lower the table so that Chester could get down easily. The mechanism creaked and groaned in protest as the unit inched its descent. Suddenly it shuddered, then stopped.

Jake stepped on the pedal again, but a grinding noise filled the air.

Chester frowned. 'Good gravy. Did I break it?'

'Afraid not. It's been threatening to quit for some time.'

'Are these tables expensive?'

Jake thought of the recent order for his own clinic.

Guilt washed over him—the ones he planned to replace were in better condition than Kirsten's. 'They're definitely an investment.'

Chester fell silent. 'Dr Holloway has a hard time making ends meet, doesn't she?'

At Jake's questioning glance he continued, 'I know the people who come here. Nearly everyone lives paycheck to paycheck, and each one hardly covers the basics. If it weren't for her, giving away medicine and so on, we'd be in trouble.

'Take me, for instance. My retirement and government checks keep me comfortable, but they just don't stretch far enough. I pay what I can, but I'm afraid that someday this clinic won't be here.'

Jake had seen enough to know that the clinic's demise was more imminent than 'someday'. Even if he continued his family's contributions the effort would be as effective as slapping a loose bandage on a torn artery. The center's life was seeping away, and something had to be done to prevent it—but what?

'Dr Holloway is committed to the center so I'm sure she'll work something out,' Jake said.

'Hope so.'

'Don't forget to come back in a month.' With the final admonition, he went in search of Amy and found her in the storage closet.

He handed Chester's chart to her. 'He's OK for another round of diuretics. Give him the same as before.'

'Will do.'

'Any more patients?'

'Not unless you'd like to give a few allergy shots and hand out baby formula.'

'I'll pass.'

Amy grinned. 'I thought so.'

'Where's Kirsten?'

Reading Chester's prescription from his chart, she spoke without looking up. 'She was in her office a few minutes ago, crunching numbers.'

'Thanks.'

He found Kirsten poring over a ledger, as Amy had said. Not wanting to disturb her, he leaned against the doorframe and folded his arms. The late afternoon sun streamed through the window, highlighting her auburn hair. Even from this distance he imagined he could smell the floral scent he now associated with her, the same scent that reminded him of springtime and his grandmother's garden.

She worried her lip with her teeth and he felt an urge to taste her mouth for himself. Her frustration was evident in the way she toyed with her bangs.

'Knock, knock,' he said, striding toward her desk. 'You need a break.'

Kirsten leaned back and rubbed her neck. 'I'll say.'

Jake glanced at the neat figures recorded on the pages. 'Problems?' he asked, already suspecting her answer.

'Only if you consider a zero balance a problem. Today seems to be the day for bad news.'

'I hate to add another brick to your load but the exam table in room one has died.'

She sighed. 'Why am I not surprised?'

'Actually, it's amazing. I didn't think antiques like that one existed except in museums.'

'Thanks a lot,' she said without rancor. 'I'll have you know we got it from—'

'A little old doctor who only used it once a week, right?'

She punched him playfully on the arm. 'I don't know about the once-a-week part, but I did buy it at an estate sale so don't laugh. It's had its problems but usually a squirt of oil takes care of the squeaks.'

'A lube job won't fix it today. Take my word, I know dead when I see it and the lift mechanism has died.'

Kirsten opened the bottom desk drawer, pulled out a spray can of lubricant and rose. ' "Oh, ye of little faith," ' she quoted.

Jake stepped aside. 'This I have to see.'

Inside the now-vacant examination room Kirsten depressed the foot pedal. The grinding noise started but the table lowered as expected. She threw him a look of triumph. 'It's all in the touch, Dr Marshall.'

Jake tried the pedal for himself. This time the head portion moved as he'd wished. 'I guess.'

'Let this be a lesson to you. Don't be so quick to sign the death certificate.'

A strange odor caught Jake's attention. He sniffed, recognizing the characteristic scent that hot electrical wires emitted.

'What's that smell?' She glanced toward the trash can.

Jake crouched down next to the table and unplugged the cord. 'It's coming from here. Now do you believe me?'

'I suppose.' Her tone was resigned.

He straightened, sorry to see the disappointment written on her face. 'Do you know what you need?'

'An electrician?'

Jake shook his head. 'An Orange Julius drink.'

'I beg your pardon?'

He hesitated at her incredulous expression. It had been a long time since he'd invited a woman out on such short notice. Truthfully, his time was always scheduled down to the minute with patient appointments and board meetings. 'I hear they're delicious. I've never had one, myself.'

'Are you serious?'

God, he must have lost his touch. He nodded. 'I've seen the last patient so there's no reason we can't sneak away a little early.'

Kirsten laughed. 'Trying to teach me your bad habits?'

He shrugged. 'When opportunity knocks. . .'

'I haven't made my hospital rounds yet.'

'Neither have I,' he said. 'I won't keep you more than an hour, I promise.'

She brushed at her bangs. 'I shouldn't.'

Seeing the longing on her face and sensing her capitulation, he tugged off his tie and unbuttoned his collar. 'Get your coat. I don't want to waste a minute.'

'If you've never tasted an Orange Julius what made you think of it?' Kirsten sipped the foamy liquid through a straw, savoring the tangy orange taste as much as she relished the sight of a relaxed Jake.

'One of our patients, Chester Olsen, recommended it. Said that he and his wife always had one.'

She liked the way he said 'our patients'. 'Chester's a nice man.'

'Doesn't he have any family to look after him? A son or daughter?'

'I don't think so. Why?'

He shrugged. 'He had the hem of his pants *stapled*.'

'It holds better than masking tape. Besides, you've seen worse.'

'Yes,' he began, appearing thoughtful, 'but it seemed to make more of an impression on me today. While he was there I had this strange feeling of being superimposed on Chester's life—staples and all.'

Kirsten ran her tongue over her teeth. 'I don't think you need to worry.'

His eyes became searching. 'What makes you say that?'

'You can sew.'

He blinked, then laughed as he caught her meaning.

Kirsten grinned. 'See? You need to lighten up. Relax and do more spur-of-the-moment things.'

'Says the woman who didn't want to come.'

She waved aside his comment. 'We're not discussing my habits. As a rule, your career comes first, doesn't it?'

'Usually, but not always. I golf.'

'Yes, but, if memory serves, don't you have to *schedule* a tee-off time in order to play?'

'I see your point.' Jake glanced at his watch. 'Since I promised not to keep you for more than an hour I'd better take you back.'

With keen disappointment, Kirsten shrugged herself into her parka and snapped it closed. She couldn't recall when an hour had passed as quickly as this one had.

As they left the comfort of the mall to brave the elements once again Kirsten gritted her teeth to keep them from chattering. 'Brr, it's cold. Hot chocolate would have been a better choice.'

'We'll get that next time.'

Anticipation made her pulse race.

He motioned ahead of them. 'Watch out for the ice.'

Before she could sidestep the patch he'd indicated Jake grabbed her elbow. Hauling her close, he guided her over the slick spot.

In spite of the layers of winter-wear separating them, Kirsten could still feel his hard frame. For those few steps she enjoyed having his arm around her waist, holding her hip against his.

Her delight continued as he maintained his grip even after he had successfully navigated past the perceived danger. 'Parking lots can be so treacherous in the winter,' he remarked, speaking in her direction. His warm breath caressed her cold cheek. 'Especially at night.'

'I agree.' Her voice sounded raspy and she cleared her throat. 'I'm ready for summer.'

'Ah, yes. Good old one-hundred-degree heat, mosquitoes and sunstroke.'

'The smell of freshly cut grass, the sound of kids playing baseball in one of the vacant lots, the clear evening skies when you can pick out every constellation,' she corrected.

'The only one I could ever find was the Big Dipper.' He stopped next to his Jeep. 'Come to think of it, I haven't done that since I was a kid.'

She snuggled under his arm and stared into his face. 'See what you've been missing?'

His mouth curved into a lopsided grin and his eyes shone with devilment. 'I'm about to find out.'

Before she could interpret his remark he sandwiched Kirsten between himself and his vehicle, cupped her chin with one hand and pressed his lips against hers.

Jake's hand warmed her cold skin but the heat from his mouth created an inner fire hotter than a blue flame. No outside source could possibly have raised her core temperature any faster or higher.

With the full length of his body compressed against hers, she flung her arms around his chest and wished away the thick barrier of his coat and her parka.

Falling under the spell, her lips parted. She tasted the tangy orange—smelled the citrus scent mingling with his—and felt the rough stubble on his face grating against her cold cheeks. Her knees wobbled.

Jake lifted his head, far enough to break contact but still close enough for his breath to touch her now-heated skin.

Kirsten blinked. 'What was that for?'

His face showed a distinct degree of satisfaction. 'You said I needed to do more spur-of-the-moment things. I decided to find out what I'd been missing.'

He'd turned her words but she didn't care. 'And did you?'

'Definitely.'

'Hey, you two. Come over here and stand by my car.' A man waved at them.

Jake turned toward the voice but kept his arm around her. 'What's up, Roy?'

Roy grinned. 'You're defrosting your windows. I'd like for you to do mine next.'

Jake laughed. 'Not a chance.' With that, he unlocked the passenger door and boosted Kirsten inside. He hurried to the driver's seat and started the engine. 'I'd have introduced you to my partner, Roy, but it's too cold to be standing in the wind.'

'We were,' she pointed out.

'Kissing is different. Wouldn't you agree?'

Still enjoying the after-effects of their heated embrace, she grinned.

'Would you mind if I stopped by my office? Seeing Roy reminded me that I need to pick up a few charts to review.'

In no hurry to part company, Kirsten nodded. The five days until Tuesday—her next opportunity to see Jake— seemed five days too long.

After maneuvering through traffic for several miles he rounded the corner and pulled into an alleyway running in a north-south direction. 'Not the grandest entrance but it's the closest.'

Noticing the parking stall with his name, she recognized the rear side of the building. Even in the darkness she could see evidence of construction: piles of dirt and a chain-link fence surrounding stacks of lumber and other supplies.

He pointed to a pillar a few steps away from the non-assuming entrance. 'Posts like this one marked the original corners, but since we've added onto both ends we've incorporated the columns in our design.'

Security lights in strategic places near the foundation and along the eaves glowed like beacons in the night, allowing her to see the entire structure. 'My gosh, you've doubled the size.'

'Almost.'

Reaching behind his seat, he grabbed a thin briefcase before he jumped out of his vehicle. She followed suit, anxious to see the interior. Once inside, the smell of sawdust and fresh paint filled the air. Before she could comment he led her down a corridor and unlocked a door sporting his nameplate.

Jake flicked a light switch and Kirsten found herself in his waiting-room. Decorated in masculine shades of gray and blue with an occasional accent of burgundy, the area seemed warm and inviting. His chairs were cushioned, covered in rich-looking navy fabric and designed for comfort—a far cry from the folding chairs she provided for her own clients.

She followed him through his domain, taking in the receptionist's office with its metal files containing color-coded patient records, desks holding computer terminals and fax machines plus a variety of other office equipment.

Although the smell of sawdust lingered she saw no evidence of construction invading this area. 'I thought you were remodeling.'

'I'm the last one on the list. We decided to build the new wing first, move the pediatrics group into it and then redo their old offices before another practice moved in.' He hesitated. 'Unfortunately, we ran into problems and things got delayed. We've worked them out, but it put us behind schedule.

'So, to save time, we rearranged our schedules and consolidated offices as much as we could. I share my space with whoever is undergoing renovation, which is why I have a few days off each week for the next several months.'

He flung open another door. 'This is my private study. The exam rooms are all along this hallway. Feel free to poke around. It'll take me a few minutes.'

Left alone, Kirsten turned the first doorknob she came to. With a flick of a switch she banished the darkness and revealed an exam table much newer than hers and light blue counter-tops that gleamed. She couldn't resist studying his table—the unit responded to the foot pedal controls with ease and little sound. The wallpaper's speckled pattern co-ordinated with the paper on the walls of the hallway and waiting area.

She meandered into the next cubicle. It, too, was decorated to complement the other rooms. For a brief moment she wondered what it would be like to work in such beautiful surroundings.

Although she didn't begrudge Jake his success, the differences between her clinic and his glared at her as sharply as the differences between night and day. She found only one similarity—the odor of disinfectant.

Another hard truth came upon her—she was as

out of place in his world as he was in hers.

Did he dread each Tuesday and Thursday? Consider his hours at the Family Health Center as time spent in the Dark Ages? One thing was certain—he didn't have someone like Carlton breathing down his neck, making him wonder how he'd make the next rent payment for a building that needed more repairs than it was worth.

With her mood dimmed, she shut off the lights and closed the door. Ignoring the other rooms, she strolled back to Jake's private study and found him holding swatches of wall-coverings at arm's length.

'What do you think?' He placed them on top of his credenza and took a step backward, cocking his head to study each piece from another angle.

The floral print didn't suit him. Finally she selected one. 'The jagged stripe is nice.'

He stared at it another moment before nodding. 'The stripe it is.'

'Er, don't you think you should get your office help's opinion?' she asked uneasily. 'After all, they'll stare at it every day. I won't.' The thought pained her for reasons she didn't want to think about.

'I did. They narrowed it down to these three. I cast the deciding vote.'

'Of course, I don't see anything wrong with what you already have.'

'Neither do I, but I'm moving into the suite next door. We're also knocking out a few walls to make our medical records area larger.'

While he gathered another sheaf of papers and stuffed them into his bulging briefcase Kirsten sauntered around the room. She noticed his original Norman Rockwell print of a boy in a doctor's waiting-room anxiously awaiting his turn, the expensive oak desk, the matching credenza and bookcase. A model of the human heart stood sentry on one shelf, residing between two book-ends holding tomes of cardiac medicine and a physician's desk reference.

It could have been any physician's office, but the residual scent made it Jake's and no other's.

He glanced around one last time. 'I think I have every-thing. Are you ready?'

'Whenever you are.' She tried to sound brighter than she felt.

Within minutes they were in his Jeep and on their way once again.

'You're quiet,' he said as he negotiated the turns to enter the expressway.

How could she explain that she had foolishly forgotten that Jake's lifestyle was the exact opposite of her own? That they were poles apart—as different as the city and country mice in the children's story. 'Just tired. The day's catching up to me.'

Jake drove the remaining miles in silence. As he approached her section of town the homes lining the streets took on a beaten appearance. Her building loomed ahead in the darkness, illuminated only by Jake's head-lights.

She stole a glance at him, memorizing his features as it would be Tuesday before she saw him again. 'Thanks for the Orange Julius and for showing me your clinic.'

He smiled. 'Any time.'

As he drew closer to the structure she motioned to a curbside parking space. 'Let me off here.'

'You're not going home?'

'Paperwork never ends,' she quipped. 'I still have a few numbers to crunch.'

He gestured to her right. 'From the looks of things,

you're not the only one working late.'

A faint glow came from the side window near Irene's office. 'Irene doesn't like to leave her job undone.'

Jake rolled the Jeep to a complete stop and she hopped out of the vehicle. 'Thanks again for everything,' she said, before slamming the door closed and hurrying to the front entrance.

He waited until she'd unlocked the door and waved before he pulled away.

Even with the radio blaring, the twenty-minute drive to his home seemed almost lonely. It was unbelievable how Kirsten's presence had made such an impact that he felt her absence so keenly.

Jake parked in his garage and shut off the engine. Reaching in the back seat for his briefcase, his gaze landed on a billfold lying half-hidden on the floor.

He reached for it, certain of its owner's identity. The driver's license inside confirmed his suspicions and he wondered if Kirsten had discovered it missing.

A slow grin crossed his face. The opportunity to see her again after such a short separation was perfect. She couldn't drive without her license, not if she wanted to avoid problems with the local law enforcement. The prospect of returning it held more appeal than the briefcase of medical documents awaiting his attention.

Without another thought, he backtracked to her clinic. This time, as he drove past the front entrance, he was disappointed to see that the windows were dark. Obviously, she'd gone home some time during the past forty minutes. If only he'd written down the clinic's telephone number and called ahead of time. But he hadn't, and his earlier elation quickly changed to disappointment.

As he inched to a stop at the intersection a sense of foreboding came over him. The street seemed different, almost sinister, and it didn't take long to ascertain why the night lay like a heavy blanket.

The lamp on the opposite corner wasn't shining.

He glanced at the top of the pole. Only a jagged edge of the globe remained in place. Pieces of glass littered the ground, shining in the scattered beam of his head-lights like giant pieces of ice on an already snow-packed sidewalk.

Kirsten's earlier assurances echoed in his memory— 'We haven't been robbed in over a year. Word must have gotten out that we don't have anything of street value.'

Immediately he shifted gear and drove to the center's parking lot. Kirsten's car and one other—a battered Chevy that he didn't recognize—were there, and he sensed that the owner hadn't dropped in for a medical consultation.

He shifted into park mode before the Jeep had come to a complete stop, aware of only one thing.

Kirsten had stumbled into trouble.

CHAPTER SEVEN

LOCKING the door behind her, Kirsten turned in the darkness and ran into what seemed like a brick wall. This one, however, smelled of stale sweat, cigarettes and alcohol.

Before she could inhale to scream a hairy arm circled her throat and pulled her backwards. The pressure against her larynx prevented a protest.

'Well, now. Who's this?' the gruff voice in her ear demanded.

A flashlight shone in her face, blinding her. 'It's the doc.' The person's voice behind the beam squeaked in a manner characteristic of adolescent males.

'Then you're smart enough to know what we want, aren't you?'

Kirsten shuddered.

The arm against her throat tightened. 'Aren't you?'

She nodded, fear flooding her in a way she'd never imagined or experienced before. 'I don't keep anything you can use,' she croaked.

'Gimme a break, lady. This is a doctor's office and that means drugs.'

'You're wrong.'

The arm underneath her chin jerked. 'We found the penny-ante goods. Where's the rest?'

A painful muscle spasm gripped Kirsten's neck and she bit into her lip. 'That's all there is.'

'We don't believe you, Doc.' The man released his hold and she gasped for air. He clamped his hands on her upper arms, keeping her back toward him. The pressure of his grip made her grateful for the heavy coat. 'You're gonna show us your stash.'

Fear burned her throat. 'I don't have one,' she repeated. If only she hadn't sent Jake on his way—but she had. She had to keep her wits if she wanted to survive unscathed.

'Keep looking,' the man with the gruff voice ordered the boy. 'There's gotta be somethin' here we can use.' The flashlight's owner turned away and veered off in another direction.

'You,' he shoved Kirsten, 'move on.' Off balance, she stumbled. The muscular fellow—the obvious ring-leader—grabbed at her. Digging his fingers into her parka, he yanked. Fabric ripped and the snaps popped.

For once she was thankful that she hadn't repaired her broken zipper. She let the garment drop from her arms as she bolted toward the rear exit, intending to dash past the burglars and into the night.

She made it to the hallway before a vise-like grip clamped onto her wrist. Before she could pull free, her arm was twisted behind her back and she was propelled along the corridor. 'Thought you could get away, huh?'

Out of the corner of one eye she saw the glow of battery-powered lamps in two other rooms.

Oh, God, were there *three* of them?

As she was pushed forward the sound of a crash and the tinkle of glass made her wince at the unseen damage. Her eyes adjusted to the faint lighting created by the exit sign and she began to make out the shapes of familiar office landmarks.

Her captor stopped in front of the open medicine closet. She surveyed the shelves she'd restocked earlier, now empty. Pills crunched beneath her feet and bottles of liquid medication dripped their contents into dark puddles on the floor.

From what she could see, everything given out of generosity and each item she'd purchased was either missing or had been destroyed. None of her patients would benefit from her efforts, only these street-tough hoodlums.

The leader grabbed her by the scruff of her neck, making tears come to her eyes. 'Where's the rest of the goodies?'

She hunched her shoulders, trying to lessen the pain of his grip. 'This is it.'

The man shook her until her teeth seemed to rattle. 'Don't lie.'

'I'm not,' she said hoarsely, wondering why the fickle hand of fate had allowed her to run into two unsavory characters in the same day.

'What about that room?' He pointed to her office.

Before she could answer the other boy, who'd greeted her at the door, came out. 'Nuthin' in there.'

Before he moved out of her field of vision she noticed his slender build, the dark clothing and a black stocking cap covering his hair. The room's shadows and the camouflage paint smeared across his thin face obscured any salient features the youth possessed.

If only the leader would step in front of her. . . Then again, perhaps it was for her own good that she couldn't identify him.

A third voice, sounding equally young, also came from behind. 'There's nuthin' anywheres. This ain't nuthin' but a low-budget operation. Some clinic this is.' Disgust oozed from his voice.

The sweaty fellow's grip on her arm tightened like a

tourniquet. Her skin burned and her hand grew numb. 'Is that true, Doc?'

'Yes,' she cried.

'This stop has been a disappointment,' he snarled, maintaining his hold on her neck. 'But if I ever find out you weren't honest with me we'll be back. Count on it.'

She gulped and nodded.

One of the young men cocked his head and peered into her dark office. 'We oughta go, man. I saw somethin' movin' outside the window.'

Hope flickered into life.

'Check it out.' The one in charge turned to the other accomplice. 'Grab the boxes.' In the next breath his low and menacing voice drifted past Kirsten's ear.

'Remember what I said because if we don't catch you here we'll find out where you live. Got it?'

Once again she nodded.

'Just so you don't forget we mean business—'

He flung her away as if she were no more than a bothersome fly, launching her into the nearest wall. Her head cracked against the sharp corner of the wooden casement framing the entrance to her office.

Pain seared her forehead and nose as she bounced off the unyielding partition like a rubber ball and landed on the sticky floor. She vaguely heard a bellow of rage and her name, but with her mind cloaked in a dense fog she couldn't make any sense of it.

She raised one hand to her face, feeling something warm and wet covering her fingertips. Her arm tingled with thousands of tiny pin-pricks as she regained her circulation, but the fringes of gray grew darker and darker until, finally, she gave herself up to the blackness.

*   *   *

Jake clung to the side of the building, using the scraggly evergreen trees for cover as he focused on his destination—the back exit. He'd alerted the authorities from his car phone, but waiting for their arrival wasn't an option—not while Kirsten was in danger. He sneaked past the window of her office, but a glimpse of the drama inside caught his attention and he paused for a closer look.

Kirsten stood framed in the doorway off the well-lit corridor with a man's arm around her throat. Jake's stomach tensed and his anger mushroomed.

One of the men glanced in his direction and he ducked. Driven by fury, he moved closer to the door—concerned more with speed than stealth.

The lock was broken—a plus, in his opinion, since he wouldn't have to mess with a key. Ready to spring inside, he flung the door open and met one of the intruders face to face.

Black camouflage paint covered the man's features, and the whites of his widened eyes revealed his surprise. Jake's faster reflexes took over. He roared his displeasure and landed a right hook as accurately and effectively as a well-trained boxer.

The fellow crumpled against the wall and Jake rushed past, shouting Kirsten's name.

In the next instant two more men came toward him, similarly disguised and carrying boxes. Jake swung at the closest one and, from the grunt of pain, knew he'd made contact. Before he could continue his offensive attack the other shoved him off balance and the trio escaped into the night.

Regaining his footing, he hurried in the direction he'd seen Kirsten as he called her name. The echo of his voice answered, along with the sound of his own heels pounding on the linoleum. He called again. The radiators replied with a series of clangs and a familiar hiss.

Just as he entered the leg of the L-shaped corridor he found Kirsten, seated on the floor with her back against the wall. Blood was streaming down her face and dripping onto her shirt.

Thank God she was alive.

'Kirsty, can you hear me?'

Out of her pain-filled fog Kirsten heard a far-away voice. With the horror of the last few minutes etched in her mind and fearing that the sweaty man had returned, she flinched and scooted away.

The footsteps came closer. 'Kirsten, it's me.'

The soothing, masculine voice finally penetrated her haze and she recognized its owner. 'Jake,' she breathed, her adrenalin surge stabilizing as her vision came into focus.

He pressed a soft towel against her forehead to staunch the flow of blood. 'I'm right here.'

Tears of relief came to her eyes. She'd never been so glad to see anyone. 'I thought you went home.'

'I did, but you left your billfold in my car and so I came back. Good thing, too.'

Leaning her head against the wall, she stared at his welcome face. A pine fragrance foreign to him hovered in the air. Her gaze travelled upward to the pieces of greenery stuck to his hair, and she reached out to remove a fragment. 'What's this?'

'Evergreen.'

'How did you get—?' He took it from her and she saw the scrapes across his knuckles. 'And what about your hands?'

'I'm fine, but two of them left with sore jaws,' he

said, brushing a strand of hair off her cheek-bone. 'You, on the other hand, can't work alone any more. It's too dangerous.'

Hearing his vehemence, her protest died unspoken. Now wasn't the time to argue that the demands on her didn't conform to daylight hours and that a bodyguard was out of the question.

'If I'd known they were here I wouldn't have come in at all,' she said wearily, allowing him to fuss over her. 'It was a case of rotten timing.'

She glanced over his shoulder. The damage to the medicine closet brought a lump to her throat. Her precious stock of medicine was either missing or unusable. 'How bad is it?'

'You'll need a few stitches. Four or five at least.'

'Not me. The clinic.'

'They trashed the place but how badly, I can't say. I was more interested in finding you.'

Every bit of energy seemed to drain out through her toes. She sighed. In spite of her desire to weep, she dug deep and gathered the shredded pieces of her composure. Crying didn't solve anything—action did. The whole episode still didn't feel real, more like a nightmarish dream. Yet it hadn't been a fantasy—for the next few weeks, she'd wear the proof.

'I want to see for myself.'

He laid a hand on her shoulder. 'In a minute. How's the forehead?'

'Sore.'

'Are you hurt anywhere else?' Even as he spoke, he was running his hands along her extremities.

Kirsten started to shake her head, but pain stabbed her skull and she stopped. 'No.'

'Let's patch you up.' Jake gripped her arms and lifted

her to her feet. Her bruised muscles complained as she locked her knees to stand.

'What's wrong?'

She hastened to wipe away the worry on his face. 'A few aches, that's all.'

Appearing totally unconvinced, he wrapped one arm around her waist.

Although she could walk under her own power she leaned against his hard frame and accepted his support. His presence, along with his familiar scent, displaced the repulsive memory of her attacker for the time being.

The shrill call of a police siren grew louder, then stopped. She glanced at him questioningly.

'I called the cops before I came after you.'

She paused on the threshold of the first exam cubicle to survey the damage. 'Are all the rooms like this?'

'More or less,' he said, his tone noncommittal.

As she crossed the room she hoped it would be 'less'. It was bad enough losing her precious drug supply without losing equipment as well.

She sank onto the table just as two policemen walked in, wearing bomber-style jackets and the familiar hats.

'Did you stop them?' Jake asked.

The older one, with Sgt Gates printed on his black name-tag, shook his head. 'No. We think they might be the same guys who've hit other medical offices in the past few months. Don't worry, we'll catch them sooner or later.'

Kirsten's shoulders sagged. She didn't like the 'later' part.

'Any ideas on who they were?' Gates asked.

'It was dark and I couldn't see,' she said. A sudden picture of a skinny youth flashed into her mind. 'Although I might recognize the adolescent. The other two, especially the one giving the orders, stayed behind me.'

'What makes you think he was a kid?'

'His voice. It sounded like it was changing.'

'Two were teenagers,' Jake agreed. 'They didn't have the build of someone older, although the ringleader was more mature. They all had stocking caps on and their faces were blackened so I can't identify them.'

'Too bad. Still, we might pick up some fingerprints,' Officer Gates said. 'We'll also need your statements.'

'It will have to wait,' Jake interjected. 'She needs medical attention first.'

The cop studied Kirsten. 'Want us to call for an ambulance?'

'Yes,' Jake replied, his jaw set and his mood grim.

'Absolutely not.' Kirsten stiffened her spine. 'We're both physicians. We can handle minor scrapes.'

'A trip to the hospital is a good idea.' Jake's tone became placating, similar to the one she used when trying to coax a child into co-operation.

'I said no and I meant it. No ambulance.'

The two men stared at each other. Finally, Jake shrugged. 'I'll let you know.'

Although Jake had seemed to acquiesce she sensed that he was biding his time.

Officer Gates withdrew to the crime scene, closing the door behind him. Meanwhile, Jake helped Kirsten to lie down, then studied the cut on her forehead. 'Maybe I should ask Mr Olsen to run his stapler over.'

'Gee, thanks.'

He frowned, still inspecting the gash. 'Are you sure you want me to do this?'

'Better you than a medical student. Besides, you said you could sew.'

'Yeah, but nothing fancy.'

'I'm not entering a quilt exhibition. I'd stitch it myself, but it'd be tough having only one good eye and no depth perception.'

Jake grinned. 'Nice to see you haven't lost your sense of humor.'

'It's the only thing I haven't lost,' she said wryly. 'Can we get on with this?'

'Just as soon as I find a suture pack.' He rummaged through the supplies scattered across the floor. 'Ah, here's one. You're in luck. It hasn't been opened, crushed or otherwise mutilated.'

'Unlike myself.'

'Relax. I'll be finished before you can count to a hundred.'

'Twenty-five, fifty, seventy—'

'Hey,' he protested, 'that's cheating. Have to do it right. While you're at it make it two hundred.'

'Why not a thousand?'

'Better yet.'

A sharp sting seared her forehead and she bit her lower lip.

'Sorry,' he said.

'I should hope so.'

'Are you counting?'

Kirsten peered at him through her good eye. 'No.'

He poked and prodded the edges of the cut. 'You can start any time.'

His light-hearted bantering soothed her frayed nerves and she found his presence, along with his steady movements, comforting. Forcing herself to breathe deeply, she closed her eyes while Jake worked.

'There,' he said a few minutes later. 'All done. You realize that we'll have matching scars.'

'Great. Just what I wanted.' She struggled to sit up, but Jake pressed her down with a hand to her shoulder.

'Not so fast. I'm not finished.' He tugged her blouse free of her trousers and pressed on her abdomen. 'Does that hurt?'

'Not a bit.'

His doctor persona had taken over and she knew that he was more concerned than he'd first appeared. Warmed by the thought, she let him examine her ribs.

'You need a blood count and a urinalysis.'

'No, I don't. I know what to watch for, and I will. Don't worry. Just let me up.'

Clearly unconvinced, he grabbed her upper arm and brought her upright. Although his grip wasn't tight she winced. Immediately she glanced at Jake, hoping that he hadn't seen her reaction.

His fierce expression revealed that he had. 'Off with the shirt.'

'I'm bruised, that's all.'

He folded his arms, a mulish expression on his face. 'If you don't remove it I will.'

'You can't.'

'Wanna try me? I'm bigger than you.'

'Pretty poor bedside manner, if you ask me.'

'I didn't. Come on. Time's awasting.'

'I don't want to.' She sounded petulant but she didn't care. Having been victimized this evening, she needed to exert control of her life even if it meant arguing over something minor.

He gave her a give-me-a-break look. 'I promise to guard your modesty and keep all leering to a minimum. I'm a doctor, remember?'

'That's not it.' She studied her fingernails.

The paper sheet on the table crackled as he sat beside

her. 'Look,' he said, 'I know you probably aren't suffering from anything that a few days of rest won't cure.' He enfolded her hands in his. 'But I need to check for my own peace of mind.'

His sincerity, combined with the worry lines around his mouth, convinced her. She began unbuttoning her blouse. 'Just for the record, I'm only doing this for you.'

Jake stood beside her and eased the fabric off her shoulders. His utter and complete silence revealed more than mere words.

Craning her neck, she studied her upper arms—first one, then the other. Large dark blue and purple marks already mottled her skin. Jake traced her collar-bone, moving around to her spine.

'I'm still in one piece,' she joked, trying to lighten his somber mood.

'That does it. I want lab work and X-rays.' His jaw was squared, his mouth pressed into a determined line.

Pulling on her shirt and buttoning it, she shook her head. 'Please don't make more of this than it already is.'

'Sorry,' he said, 'I won't risk your health. The only choice you have is if you want your trip to the hospital in an ambulance or my car. That's it.'

The steel in his voice told her that he wouldn't relent, and she was too tired to fight him any longer. Yet she wanted to try for one more concession. 'OK, OK. I'll let you drive me. But only after the police are finished.'

He glanced at his watch. 'Twenty minutes. No more.'

'An hour.'

Jake shook his head. 'Twenty minutes.'

'Forty-five.'

'Twenty. And if you keep arguing about it we'll leave sooner, even if I have to carry you out.'

'All right,' she muttered. With mincing movements,

she stepped down. As soon as she entered the hallway Officer Gates approached and she led the way to Irene's office as it was the closest and most comfortable.

To Kirsten's surprise, the thieves hadn't left this area untouched: medical records and other secretarial supplies littered the floor.

Jake sat beside her on the couch, his mere presence providing the emotional support she needed to relive those harrowing minutes. Staring straight ahead at the blank wall with her hands clasped together, she recited the events as objectively as she could while Gates took notes.

By the time she'd finished her monologue Jake's mood had grown darker than she'd thought possible.

After hearing Jake's version, Officer Gates placed his report forms in a file. 'That's it for now. We'll need a list of the missing items as soon as possible.'

'I'll do my best,' she promised.

'We'll get back to you if anything new develops.'

Gates's partner poked his head inside. 'The lab crew's finished.'

'Me, too.' With that, the policemen left.

'Time to go,' Jake said, helping Kirsten to her feet.

'In a minute.' Anxious to survey the damage for herself, she walked through the hallways and opened every door on the way.

The thieves had left their mark everywhere. Cupboards had been emptied, shelves had been cleared— their contents scattered across the floor like autumn leaves. Bottles of alcohol and bags of saline lay on their sides, leaking into ever-widening pools.

She stared at the bare medicine closet, hoping to see her precious pharmaceuticals. Nothing, however, had changed. Only a few items at the very back had escaped the thieves' long reach.

She moved on in zombie-like strides. Jake followed.

The room which had been stocked with a miscellaneous assortment of materials and equipment now appeared as if a tornado had struck. Like the other areas, everything had been torn from the shelves. Crushed baby formula cans created a milky mess.

Words failed Kirsten. Her emotions churned with each new glimpse of wanton destruction and despair overtook her.

'A little cleaning and we'll have everything back to normal,' Jake said.

'It will take days,' she answered flatly.

'By Monday you'll be back in business.'

Her temper flared. 'With what? Shall I sort through the pills on the floor and pass those out? There isn't a syringe or needle to be found. And, even if there was, I don't have any medicine to dispense.'

He appeared unconcerned that she'd vented her anger on him. 'This is only an inconvenience. There's nothing here that can't be replaced.'

She hugged herself, feeling cold in spite of the heated building. 'Yeah, right. I'll just run out and buy whatever I need.'

'*You're* the only irreplaceable thing in this entire clinic, Kirsten. Don't ever forget it.'

She sighed. Fighting the lump in her throat, she asked, 'Aren't you going to tell me this would be a perfect time to close up shop? Call it quits?'

He didn't flinch under her gaze. 'I could. I probably should. Do you want me to?'

Her voice was quiet. 'No.'

He didn't seem surprised by her answer. 'Then I won't.'

She'd saved her office for last. Compared to the other rooms, her domain was relatively untouched. The file cabinet's drawers stood open and empty, the documents covering the floor like snowdrifts.

Her Ferris wheel picture and framed diploma hung at crooked angles, disarranged by a thief who'd obviously anticipated finding a wall safe.

For the first time in her life Kirsten doubted if she could recover from this latest setback. The battle to pursue her dream had escalated. Her defenses had been overpowered. How long could she continue the fight?

Darcy's doll lay on its side in a corner. She bent down to rescue the clown from its ignominious position and found its polka-dot dress sporting a distinct footprint.

For a crazy moment she wanted to wipe the perpetual grin off its face. There was nothing to smile about.

'Is it broken?' Jake asked.

Kirsten dusted at the footprint. 'No. Just dirty.'

The fluorescent lights overhead sputtered, then went out. The room plunged into darkness.

It was the proverbial last straw—the end of a rotten day. Clutching the clown to her chest, the tears began—first as a trickle, then a steady stream.

Jake's arms surrounded her and she stiffened. 'It's me,' he whispered.

Melting against his hard body, she sobbed until she had nothing left. He held her until the storm had passed. 'Come on. It's time to leave.'

She made no objection. As the police had secured the broken door with a length of rope, Jake found her coat and bundled her into it as if she were a child. With his arm around her waist, he ushered her through the front entrance and locked it behind them.

The detour to the hospital didn't take long and Jake's orders were carried out with record speed. 'Looks like you're OK,' he said, reviewing the radiology and laboratory reports before showing them to her. 'I'll take you home.'

'Finally,' Kirsten grumbled. But on the way to the parking lot she stopped short. 'I haven't made my rounds yet.'

'And you won't. Not tonight. If anyone needs you they know your number. We'll deal with it then.'

Since her hospitalized patients had been stable on her last check, she didn't argue as Jake took her elbow and guided her into the night. Within fifteen minutes he pulled to a stop in front of her duplex and escorted her inside.

She wasted no time in turning on a small table lamp, breathing a tremulous sigh as its soft radiance chased away the shadows.

Jake meandered into the open doorway and flicked on the overhead kitchen light.

Kirsten tugged off her coat and wondered how long it would take to overcome her sudden fear of the dark. Often called to the hospital at night, she didn't need the added distraction.

He returned to her side. 'How are you doing?'

She opened the coat closet and grabbed a hanger. 'Fine,' she said, with more enthusiasm than she felt.

The sound of her voice hadn't died away when she heard a loud bang against the back door, followed by a scratching noise.

Fear shot through her as she recalled her attacker's last threat and she screamed.

CHAPTER EIGHT

KIRSTEN covered her mouth with both hands. Her instincts clamored for escape and her gaze darted toward the front door.

She started to move but Jake threw his arms around her, preventing her flight as he pushed her into a corner and shielded her with his own body. 'Relax,' he murmured against her hair. 'Stay calm.'

Kirsten nodded, pressing her head against his chest. She was safe. Jake was here. Reciting those words like a mantra, she willed her adrenalin to a normal level. Before long the thump of his heartbeat steadied her nerves and she could think clearly enough for the muted sound of barking to intrude upon her thoughts.

Suddenly every ounce of tension evaporated. Her knees shook with relief and she began to laugh.

'Kirsten?' He sounded puzzled.

'Oh, Jake. It's Maggie, my neighbor's Labrador retriever. She loves to play catch. Whenever she knows I'm home she tosses her ball against the door and scratches so I'll come out and play.' She buried her nose in his shoulder. 'I feel ridiculous for overreacting.'

His chest reverberated with his chuckle. 'Don't. It was perfectly understandable. To be honest, I had a few bad moments myself.'

Reluctantly Kirsten stepped out of his embrace. 'I'm fine now. Thanks for the chauffeur service.'

He shrugged off his coat and tossed it over a wooden

129

rocking chair. 'If you're trying to convince me to leave it won't work. I'm staying.'

'You are?' She couldn't disguise the eagerness in her voice. 'I mean, what if someone tries to find you—?'

'I'll handle the "what ifs",' he said firmly. 'Go hop in the shower or soak in the tub. And don't argue with the doctor.'

She went. By the time she'd showered away all traces of her assailant's touch her skin was pink and smelled like roses.

Leaving the steam-filled bathroom clad in her prim flannel nightgown, a tantalizing aroma captured her attention. Her mouth watered.

She wondered what Jake had found in her cabinets to prepare and sauntered into the kitchen, securely knotting the tie of her maroon velour robe.

Jake turned away from the stove, brandishing a spatula. 'Hungry?'

'Yes.'

'I toasted a few cheese sandwiches. Your pantry doesn't give a guy a huge selection.' He placed a plate holding his culinary efforts in front of her, along with a bowl of her favorite pretzels.

'Mmm. Perfect,' she declared, savoring the smell before she took a bite. 'Just for the record, I hate to cook. I worked my way through college in the food services department, standing over a grill during lunchtime and preparing banquets on the weekends. When my friend Naomi and I roomed together in med school I did whatever I could to avoid kitchen duty.'

He plunked down two mugs of steaming hot chocolate, then returned with his own sandwich. 'My room-mate was the same. Good thing my grandmother taught me the basics or we'd have eaten every meal at the hospital.' He frowned. 'Come to think of it, we did anyway.'

'You had a room-mate? Not a house complete with maid service and a three-car garage?'

He laughed. 'Not a chance.' Glancing around the tiny kitchen, he added, 'My apartment looked a lot like this one.'

Kirsten fell silent. She and Naomi had shared this particular apartment—similar to the others in this low-rent neighborhood—before her friend found her own place.

'By the way, your landlord called.'

Her body froze. 'Carlton?'

He nodded. 'Said he'd heard about the break-in. He wants to stop by the clinic first thing in the morning.'

'Great,' she said, glumly chewing another bite of her sandwich. 'I suppose the police called him.'

'I imagine so. It is his property. He'll need to replace the door.'

'And charge me double, I'm sure.' Her appetite fled. Sighing, she dropped the half-eaten remains onto the plate. The idea of dealing with Carlton drained the last vestiges of her strength and she yawned.

Jake glanced at the east wall. 'I didn't realize it was so late or, I should say, early.'

Without looking, she knew that he'd seen her teapot-shaped clock. 'That clock doesn't work; it's more for decoration than function—matches my collection.'

His gaze travelled to the ledge above the cabinets where she displayed an assortment of kettles. She hoped he couldn't see the dust and cobwebs that had a tendency to appear in spite of her best efforts which, truthfully, didn't fall in the realm of Suzy Homemaker.

'You must like tea.'

She grinned. 'It's OK. I like the pots better.'

His watch beeped, signifying the hour. He rose, pulling her to her feet. 'Come on, Sleeping Beauty. It's late. Does the couch come with an extra blanket?'

'You don't have to stay,' she said, although she didn't really want to be alone.

'I told you before, I'm not leaving.'

Relieved by his declaration, another problem reared its head. 'The sofa mattress isn't very comfortable.' She nibbled on her lower lip. 'Mine's better.'

He cupped her face in his hands. 'Don't tempt me, Kirsty. You've had a huge shock tonight and I won't take advantage.' Stroking her mouth with his thumbs, he said, 'But I will take a rain check and I mean to collect on it in the not-so-distant future.'

A shiver of delight ran through her. 'OK.'

Dropping his hands, he grinned. 'You'd better find those blankets before I change my mind.'

She rushed to the hall closet and yanked out a set of navy blue sheets and two thermal blankets. Embarrassed by the poor condition of her spare pillows, she grabbed one of her own and hurried back to the living-room.

He tugged the bedding out of her arms and dropped the pile on the now-unfolded sofa. 'Thanks.'

'I'll help you. It will only take a minute.'

'I can manage,' he said firmly. 'Goodnight, Kirsty. Pleasant dreams.' Lowering his head, he kissed her.

His lips seemed gentler, less demanding than before, but he still roused the same heat-producing, temperature-rising response in her before he pulled away with obvious reluctance. 'Sleep well.'

Thoroughly wide awake, she walked into her bedroom, deciding not to change her habit of sleeping with the door open. Since she didn't know whether Jake would mind hearing her music, she inserted a London Festival Orchestra compact disk into the player on her nightstand and turned the volume low as strains of Pachelbel's Canon in D major drifted forth.

After clicking off the bedside lamp, she crawled into bed. Aware of Jake lying only a few feet away, however, sleep didn't come. Counting sheep didn't hold any appeal either. Instead, she thought about the man in the other room. His presence had imparted a special warmth to her home that other guests—including her best friend, Naomi, and her own mother—hadn't ever projected.

She stroked the percale fabric, worn as smooth as silk by repeated washing. It was easy to picture Jake next to her—she'd decorated in Native American designs rather than flowers and ruffles. Surprisingly enough, the design was similar to that of the wallpaper he'd chosen.

How ironic. For all their differences, their tastes were the same.

'When Dr Marshall called about the clinic being robbed, I didn't expect this.' Irene stared at the damaged door.

'Neither did I,' said Amy.

Rolling the length of rope into a tidy loop, Kirsten turned to face the two women. 'Now you know why he told you to wear old clothes.'

Amy gasped as soon as she caught sight of Kirsten. 'Omigosh. What happened to you?'

From the moment Kirsten had seen her reflection in the bathroom mirror she'd known that her appearance would raise questions and comments. The face staring back at her sported a blackening eye and a purple forehead laced with black suture threads. Even with a white gauze bandage covering the worst of it, she resembled the cover model on a 'battered woman' poster.

'Would you believe I ran into the doorway? With a little help, of course.' Minimizing the events, Kirsten told her story, and ended with how Jake had taken her home and brought her back early this morning. She was careful to leave out more specific details—like how he'd spent the night, how she'd awakened to his kiss and the smell of freshly brewed coffee and how having him in her home in the morning had seemed so domestic.

Amy and Irene moved from room to room, their movements slow, their faces dazed and their attitudes resigned. Although Kirsten had witnessed the destruction last night, the same damage seen in daylight seemed far worse than she remembered.

She drew a deep breath and squared her shoulders. 'As you can see, we have a lot of work to do.'

Amy sniffled and Irene's eyes glistened.

'Amy and I will clean the exam areas first in case we get an emergency.' Kirsten addressed Irene. 'Why don't you reschedule as many of our appointments as you can?'

Amy went in search of a broom while Irene left for the receptionist's area. A few seconds later Kirsten heard her shout, followed by a rapid volley of Spanish.

Amy tore around the corner and stopped short next to Kirsten. 'What in the world—?'

'I think she found the mess in her office.' Kirsten studied the cubicle that she and Jake had used. 'Salvage whatever you can. The rest. . .' Her voice died. There was no need to explain the obvious.

The two cleaned in silence until the room fairly sparkled. 'It doesn't seem to be taking as long as I'd thought,' Amy commented, sweeping the discards into a dustpan and dumping the mini-load into a giant-sized black trash bag.

'Only because we're throwing everything away.'

Kirsten's heart ached over the quantity of broken supplies. To compensate, she rejoiced for every undamaged article she found. A few needles, several vials of novocaine and epinephrine, and several cartons of latex gloves were among the few things that had remained intact.

Just as she scrawled the last much-needed item on her yellow legal-sized tablet a baritone broke the silence. 'Quite the pair of busy bees in here,' Jake said, dropping a medium-sized box on the counter.

Kirsten glanced up. Seeing the familiar form, a huge smile broke across her face and her heart rate speeded up. 'Jake! I didn't expect you until later. Much later.'

'What good is being the boss if you can't occasionally pull rank and delegate?'

'I'm glad you came.' Threading her arm through his, she studied his appearance—conscious of the changes he'd made since she'd seen him a few hours ago. The whiskery shadow on his face was gone and so were the rumpled clothes.

Used to his suit-and-tie professional appearance, the blue denim jeans, red and navy long-sleeved rugby shirt and hiking boots presented a breathtaking sight. The snug fabric across his thighs, the wide stripe accentuating his broad chest and the dusting of dark hair at his throat enhanced the virile picture.

'We definitely need muscle,' Amy said, dragging the trash bag into the hallway. 'Since we've straightened out this disaster area I'll start someplace else.'

'Avoid Irene for the time being,' Jake advised. 'I said hello and she waved her arms, muttering something in Spanish. I don't think it was a compliment.'

'I will.' Amy disappeared into the room across the hall.

In the next instant Jake lifted one taped edge of Kirsten's bandage.

'Inspecting your handiwork?' she asked.

'You bet. How's the head?'

'It aches a little. Nothing serious.'

He reaffixed the gauze pad.

'Don't you have patients to see?'

'Roy and Scott volunteered to cover for me after I explained the situation. I'm concerned about my newest case, though.'

'Oh?'

'I had a feeling that she wouldn't follow my expert advice so I specifically came to keep tabs on her.' He glanced around the cubicle. 'From the looks of things, I was right.'

Her face warmed. 'I didn't work alone. In fact, Amy cleaned most of it.'

'Regardless, your role for the rest of the day is strictly supervisory. You're not allowed to handle anything heavier than that.' He motioned toward the box.

She moved toward the carton and began lifting the flaps. 'What did you bring?'

'A few things I thought you could use—syringes, alcohol—basic stuff. My secretary is making some phone calls to see if she can round up anything else. By noon you should be somewhat functional, at least more so than you are now.'

His generosity left her speechless. How had she ever thought that self-centeredness and greed ruled his life? 'You don't know what this means to me.'

He shed a benevolent smile upon her. 'I have a good idea,' he said in a low murmur. In the next breath he asked, 'Has Carlton shown up yet?'

Before Kirsten could answer Amy stuck her head in the door and rolled her eyes. 'He just walked in. Where do you want to see him?'

Kirsten quirked one eyebrow. 'You don't really want me to answer that, do you?' She turned to Jake. 'Here I go. Wish me luck.'

Jake's eyebrows formed a dark line. 'What for? You don't owe him any apologies.'

'No, but I'm sure Carlton will blame me for something.' Instinctively she pressed on her stomach to quiet the butterflies.

Squaring her shoulders, she strode into the hallway and saw the man she considered to be the bane of her existence. 'Robert. So good of you to drop by.'

If the landlord noticed the lack of warmth in her voice he gave no indication. Nor did he acknowledge her obvious injuries.

'I saw the door,' Carlton began without preamble. 'Do you have any idea what it's gonna cost me to replace?'

'No,' Kirsten said, 'but I'm certain it won't be cheap.'

Carlton shook his finger in her face. ''Course not. I gotta hire a carpenter, too, and they charge an arm and a leg.'

He brushed past Kirsten as he strode down the hallway to peer into each room. Kirsten glanced at Jake and shrugged before she followed Carlton, being careful to stay upwind of his cloying cologne.

Carlton turned toward her. 'You're responsible for the damages.'

'I don't understand why,' Kirsten said, struggling to keep her voice even. 'This was beyond my control. I didn't have anything to do with the break-in.'

Carlton's eyes narrowed. 'The police told me what

those guys were after. If you didn't keep drugs on the premises crooks wouldn't be interested in the place.' He puckered his mouth. 'Face it, Doc. Your business is an attractive nuisance.'

Carlton's logic astounded her. How could he possibly consider her profession in the same way as unfenced swimming pools, vacant buildings and other sites that invited reckless activity?

'In my book, that makes you accountable.'

Kirsten's temper rose but she steeled herself not to vent it. 'I disagree. Unfortunately, things like this happen. Since you're responsible for repairs—'

Carlton waved his hands. 'Only on normal wear and tear. The tenant is liable for any destruction he's caused.'

She clenched her teeth until her jaw ached. 'But I didn't do this.'

Carlton straightened his tie with the mustard-yellow sunflowers on a black background. 'I'm not gonna argue about it. All I know is that I didn't do it either. Breaking and entering isn't anywhere close to the same as ordinary use or a natural act of God.'

Jake stepped forward. 'So you feel a doctor's office invites trouble.'

Carlton's head bobbed up and down.

'Well,' Jake drawled, 'if you wanted to protect your property why haven't you arranged for exterior lighting or a security system?'

Carlton's eyes narrowed into slits. 'Diana Morrison didn't bother about stuff like that.'

Kirsten knew why. Diana hadn't been able to afford such measures and Carlton didn't invite his tenants to offer suggestions. Those that were made were usually ignored or discounted.

'Seems to me I didn't have problems when she was around.'

'I wonder why,' Kirsten muttered under her breath.

Carlton's tight fist was legendary, but she hadn't realized the extent of his selfishness. How ironic that she'd avoided individuals who ranked money higher than people and had ended up renting from one.

'In any case. . .' Carlton consulted the notepad in his shirt pocket '. . .I have a rough estimate right here.' He tore off a sheet and handed it to Kirsten.

The figures recorded were astronomical, at least in her opinion. Her breath caught.

Jake tugged the scrap out of her hand to glance at it. Although his face remained congenial, his voice possessed a deadly calm element. 'A little steep, wouldn't you say?'

Carlton shrugged. 'You get what you pay for.'

'Isn't the building insured for damages?' Jake asked.

'Not that it's any of your business, but if I file a claim my rates will go up. Besides, I have to pay my deductible amount before the insurance company will fork over any money.'

'Regardless, repairs must be made and I refuse to pay for them.' Kirsten pointed to the paper in Jake's hand. 'I've been robbed once, and I won't be robbed again.'

Carlton's attitude turned black and menacing. 'If you're accusing me—'

She held her ground. 'A replacement door can't possibly cost as much as you've indicated.'

'Well, Ms Holloway. Don't think you can bring someone in to fix it for you. In case you've forgotten, I approve all repairs made to my property.'

'In other words, Kirsten couldn't possibly hire anyone who would meet your high standards. Is that correct?'

Carlton glared at Jake but didn't respond to his challenge. 'So, Doc, that leaves you with two choices. You can either pay it in full, or I'll tack the cost onto your rent each month. Plus interest, of course.'

'Of course.' Kirsten didn't bother to hide her sarcasm.

'Let's see, your payment should be about. . .' Carlton paused for a few seconds before he named a figure.

She felt as if she were falling through space. 'That's double what I'm paying now. You know I can't afford that.'

Carlton shrugged, appearing totally unconcerned.

'I wonder what the Housing Authority would say about your business practices,' Jake mentioned in an offhand tone.

Carlton bristled like a porcupine. 'Are you threatening me?'

Out of the corner of one eye Kirsten saw Amy and Irene approach, although they remained in the background.

'Not at all,' Jake answered smoothly. 'Just thinking out loud.'

The landlord straightened the lapels of his jacket. 'I've been thinking too. Renting to Dr Holloway is a real hassle—more trouble than it's worth, actually.' He rubbed his chin.

A sense of foreboding spread over Kirsten. She glanced at Jake, who continued to stare at Carlton in disgust.

'Yup.' Carlton nodded for emphasis. 'I don't want you in my building any more.'

'What?' Kirsten and Jake spoke in unison.

Carlton ran one hand over his greased-back hair, as if checking for loose strands. 'You heard me.'

She froze, unable to assimilate the repercussions

of losing their office space. 'You can't!'

'Watch me. Check the fine print on your contract. I can terminate the agreement with sixty days' notice. Starting today, I'm counting down.' Carlton turned on his heel. 'Oh, and don't forget next month's payment. The increase I told you about earlier is still in effect.'

He walked through the rear exit, slamming the door behind him. Without an operational latch, it banged several times before coming to a stop.

Kirsten swallowed. Stunned, she sagged against one wall. The Family Health Center had always tottered on a slippery edge. Yesterday's robbery and Carlton's greed had now pushed it over the edge. She had always been afraid of something like this, but now that it had happened she felt empty. Unbalanced.

Amy and Irene joined Kirsten and Jake. For a few seconds no one spoke. Finally Amy broke the silence. 'At least we won't have much to move.'

'I'm glad he won't be our landlord any more.' Irene spoke with emphasis.

'We wanted to find another place anyway,' Amy added.

Kirsten straightened and managed to smile. 'You're right, we did. We'll just have to locate one sooner than I'd anticipated.' She clapped her hands. 'Come on, gang. We have work to do and I have patients to see at the hospital.'

She started to move away but Jake touched her wrist, his demeanor apologetic. 'I shouldn't have said anything. I'm sorry.'

'It wasn't your fault. Carlton has always been difficult, more so with me than Diana. I think he's wanted us out of here for a long time.' Especially since she hadn't agreed to his little 'arrangement'. 'Why else would he charge more and do less?'

'Because he's a bum?'

Kirsten laughed. 'That, too. Don't worry, everything will work out. Who knows? This is probably a blessing in disguise.'

'So you're back to looking at the cup as half-full.'

'It's better than half-empty.'

His eyes shone with appreciation. 'You know something? You're the only woman I know who can bounce back from adversity so quickly.'

She wanted to admit that she wasn't strong; that curling up in a corner and crying over the unfairness of it was appealing; that her frustration level had reached an all-time high. Instead, she faked a groan. 'Please. Don't say "bounce". It makes my head hurt.'

But as the days passed Kirsten began to doubt her ability to recover from their latest setback. Carlton had replaced the door, gleefully reminding her that she'd pay for it one way or another.

She spent every spare moment hunting for a new location, but her efforts were unproductive. The buildings in her price range didn't meet the health center's needs and those that did exceeded her tight budget.

It was depressing.

Yet her last patient on a Thursday afternoon two weeks later brought a ray of sunshine along with his injured wrist. 'I hear you're looking for a new place,' fifty-four-year-old Phil Morgan said.

His comment yanked her attention off the preliminary radiology report. 'Yes, I am.'

'My soon-to-be ex-brother-in-law has a building a few blocks over that he needs to sell. He and my sister have been married for twenty-five years and now they're getting a divorce.' Phil shook his head. 'Hard to believe. Never dreamed they had a problem.'

'That's too bad.' It seemed such a waste for a couple who had weathered the storms of life for so many years to split up, but it happened. Someday, if she ever married—a picture of Jake flashed in her mind—she wanted it to be like the vows said, 'Till death do us part'. Just like her parents.

'Anyway,' he continued, 'if you're interested, drop by on your way home. Herb's been working late most nights, repairing a few things before he lists it with a realtor, so he'll be there.'

Although she hadn't intended to stretch her meager finances to an outright purchase, the advantages of owning her own place paraded by in her mind.

Making a quick decision, Kirsten said, 'I'd like to look at it.'

Phil quoted the address and his brother-in-law's phone number while she jotted them on her prescription notepad. 'I drive by there every night so I'll stop and let him know you're coming.'

Satisfied with the arrangement, she focused on her patient and his swollen joint. 'The X-rays don't show anything broken. Can you tell me what happened?'

'My wife's been after me to knock a wall out between the kitchen and dining-room. I guess swinging a sledgehammer all day when I'm not used to manual labor wasn't too smart,' he said ruefully.

'Not when you consider that it will take about six weeks to cure the tendinitis.'

'Six weeks?' He was aghast.

'Give or take. In the meantime, use a heating pad or a hot compress but be careful you don't burn yourself.

Also take an over-the-counter pain-reliever as needed.'

Phil nodded his understanding and Kirsten continued, 'I'll put a splint on your wrist to immobilize the arm. The best thing for tendinitis is rest so wielding a hammer is out of the question.'

The man's eyes twinkled. 'Are you sure you can't use a cast instead? If my wife thinks it's broken she won't fuss at me so much.' He leaned closer. 'I didn't want to tackle this project in the first place, and she knows it.'

Kirsten smiled. 'Sorry.' As soon as she'd affixed the removable splint she sent him on his way.

Jake met her in the hallway. 'What's the plan for this evening? Another office-hunting expedition?'

'You bet. One of my patients gave me a lead,' Kirsten said. 'I'm going to meet the owner on my way home, which happens to be right now.'

'Mind if I tag along?'

'I suppose you can, but do you really want to?'

'And miss escorting my esteemed colleague around town? Not a chance.'

Although she'd have loved to have had Jake's company she hesitated. His approval meant a lot to her, but her world was one hundred and eighty degrees opposite to his. 'The places I've seen haven't been pieces of prime real estate,' she warned.

'That's OK. I'd rather look at my passenger than an old building anyway.'

Certain that her face had turned a rosy hue, she simply said, 'I'll grab my coat.'

From the looks of the structure located at the address she'd been given, vandals had taken advantage of its emptiness. Graffiti covered the bricked exterior of the former storefront building, and the number of broken windows suggested that someone had practiced his or her pitching ability with amazing accuracy.

She rang the buzzer and a voice yelled, 'Come in.' The door was unlocked so she stepped inside the foyer, with Jake right behind.

Herb Weller, a man who was obviously Phil Morgan's contemporary, met them at the door. A smile wreathed his dusty face. Sawdust, along with different shades of paint spatters, covered his overalls and red plaid flannel shirt. He offered his welcome and began to define every attribute of his property from its location to its solid construction.

'I rented the space to a small discount store until the national chain went out of business. Unfortunately, the building's been vacant ever since. Hard to keep those darn kids from doing damage. I'm willing to let it go for next to nothing.'

Unfortunately, his idea of next to nothing didn't coincide with Kirsten's. She strolled around the open space to mull over his price, the hard soles of her low-heeled shoes clicking on the tile floor and creating an eerie echo.

In her mind she visualized a waiting-room in pastel colors with cushioned chairs to match. Irene's office would be directly ahead. 'Think of all the exam rooms we could have,' she told Jake as he ambled beside her. 'Four—no, six—rooms to accommodate our patients. We'd have a huge medicine closet and several store-rooms. Your office could be next to mine, unless you'd rather have it at the other end.'

'You mean, my successor's office.'

For a second she'd forgotten that Jake wasn't a perma-nent member of the clinic. Her excitement dimmed. 'Right.'

This time she studied the building as it was—the way

Jake saw it. A pile of newspaper lay in one corner, shredded by the tiny teeth of mice into a cozy home for the resident rodents. Bird droppings dotted the floor underneath exposed rafters. From behind the remaining ceiling panels came the soft coo of a family of doves enjoying their shelter.

'This is a remodeler's dream,' Herb interjected. 'No walls to knock out. You can put anything you want wherever you want it as easy as one, two, three.'

'What's the cost to turn this into something the Health Center could use?' Jake asked. 'Just a ballpark figure.'

Herb scratched his thinning pate before he named a sum. 'That's a low guesstimate, mind you. Depends on how fancy you want everything.'

The amount he rattled off the top of his head upset Kirsten's confidence. Money like that was out of the question. Even if she persuaded the bank to grant a loan she still needed a way to pay it back. The place had potential, but it was out of her financial league.

She thanked Herb for his time and strode outside into the littered street and fresh air.

Jake guided her to his Jeep with one hand at the small of her back. 'I know you're disappointed, but there'll be other places.'

She nodded, although she despaired of ever finding something suitable. Reality, in the form of this run-down building and the well-dressed man beside her, hit her between the eyes. For the past few weeks she'd allowed herself to forget Jake's other life—his successful life. But now, facing eviction and unable to establish a base of her own, she couldn't.

Including Jake in her dream had been pure and simple foolishness. In a few months' time he would be spending his days immersed in cardiac problems and enjoying his own state-of-the-art high-tech facility, never giving a thought to the woman who operated on a shoe-string budget.

And he would never know that the same woman who could barely keep her business afloat—who anticipated each Tuesday and Thursday—had foolishly fallen in love with him.

CHAPTER NINE

'KIRSTEN? Are you OK?'

The snap of Jake's fingers brought her out of her daze and she quickly composed herself. 'I'm fine.'

'You looked strange there for a minute.'

Her grin was weak. 'I was just thinking. Actually, I might know someone who could help us.'

'Who?'

Kirsten explained about the anonymous donor, finishing with, 'Maybe I could persuade him to change his mind.'

Jake pulled into the flow of traffic. 'How do you propose to do that if you don't know who he is?'

'I'll go through the bank.'

'I'm sure this person had a good reason for his decision,' he said slowly, as if weighing his words. 'He, or she, may have unexpected financial problems of his own to sift through. Tell me something. If this person rescinded his cancellation notice would his contribution make a real difference or only provide a temporary fix?'

Jake's comment struck home. 'I'm not complaining, but it didn't stretch as far as I would have liked,' she finally admitted. 'However, every little bit helped. It was true then, and it's true today.'

'What about your other fund-raising efforts?'

She drew a deep breath. 'I've visited with several church groups. Their community service committees have supplied us with baby formula, diapers and over-the-counter children's medication. Unfortunately,

148

rent and salaries present the real worries.'

Jake turned the corner into the parking area and stopped beside Kirsten's car. 'You could join my clinic. We can always use a good family practitioner.'

'Are you serious?'

'Yes.'

'It wouldn't work, you know.'

A puzzled frown worked its way across his face. 'Why not?'

'The majority of my patients can't pay. Eventually, I'd drain your resources and the others in your practice would mutiny.'

'You don't know that.'

'It's a moot point, anyway. Your clinic doesn't qualify as an underserved area, which is a condition of my med school loan agreement. I'll have to relocate. Western Kansas is always looking for physicians.'

He appeared startled, as if that possibility had never occurred to him. 'Maybe I can call in a few favors for you,' he said.

His comment about temporary fixes suddenly sparked an idea. 'No.' She shook her head for added emphasis. 'You're right. Asking for favors won't solve anything in the long run. I've been relying on last-minute bail-outs and stopgap measures for some time and it hasn't worked. I need another plan.'

'You have something in mind?'

She hesitated, hating to divulge her idea since she doubted that Jake would approve. 'Sort of, but I don't know if I can arrange it.'

She reached over and touched his hand, enjoying the strength his fingers exuded. But before he could ask questions that she wasn't prepared to answer she hopped out of his Jeep. 'Thanks again. See you next week.'

By the time Jake had driven away she was on the phone, trying to set the wheels in motion.

Arriving at the nurses' station in Lakeside Memorial's Emergency Room on Sunday evening, Jake blinked as if he couldn't trust his eyesight. 'What are you doing here?'

'I'm covering ER. What does it look like?' In spite of Kirsten's snappy, nonchalant comeback, her heart fluttered with nervousness and her hands trembled as she flipped through the pages of a medical chart.

She'd expected the question ever since she'd placed a call to him via his answering service a short time ago, although she would have preferred to discuss her latest scheme on Tuesday. Unfortunately, this patient ruined her plans.

He raised his eyes. 'I gathered that. I don't understand why.'

She studied him in the same manner as someone looking above reading glasses, although she didn't have any. 'Surely I don't have to spell it out.'

'Never mind. Forget I said anything,' he muttered.

'My friend, Naomi, arranged for me to cover on the weekends. As you know, I can use the income.'

Without waiting for his endorsement, she skirted the counter and headed for the area where Jake's patient waited. As Jake fell into step beside her she handed him the medical record and summarized her findings in a crisp tone. 'Acute myocardial infarction. Blood tests and the EKG confirm it.'

Jake peered at her in the manner of a man biding his time before he glanced through the documents.

She whipped the curtains aside, ignoring the scratch of metal rings against the metal rod. Inevitable confrontation or not, she was thrilled to see him.

The patient, fifty-five-year-old John Tipton, appeared apprehensive, pale and in obvious pain as he lay on the gurney. His hospital gown covered the EKG leads fixed to his chest, and his hand with the IV rested across his abdomen. 'Sorry to bother you, Dr Marshall,' he croaked over the soft whir of equipment.

'No problem, John,' Jake said, his attention fixed on the screen's wavy lines. 'Looks like you've had a minor malfunction.' Speaking to Kirsten, he said, 'Call CCU and see if they have a bed.'

'I notified them about ten minutes ago. They'll be here as soon as they can to take Mr Tipton upstairs.'

'Good.' He addressed his patient. 'How's the pain?'

'It's easing some.'

Jake flipped through the pages again. 'Looks like Dr Holloway has started all the right medication. You've been in good hands.'

Kirsten breathed a sigh of relief. His praise meant a lot to her.

He snapped the folder closed. 'Let's get you settled for the night.'

A nurse and an orderly wearing rose-colored scrub suits walked in and flanked the bed. 'CCU's ready for you, Mr Tipton,' the nurse said. 'Just relax and enjoy the ride.'

As the group proceeded toward the hallway Kirsten stepped aside to allow them room, noticing that Jake did the same. He remained silent until the nursing personnel passed out of earshot. 'Don't leave. We have to talk.'

Her shift didn't end for several more hours, but she didn't bother to explain. 'I'll be here.'

As time wore on she caught herself scrutinizing every dark-haired male who entered the emergency department. Chiding herself for her actions, she took advantage of a sudden lull to slip into the staff lounge.

She had no sooner stirred the instant chocolate powder into a mug containing hot water when the door opened and Jake strode in, looking like a thundercloud. 'What do you think you're doing?'

Being deliberately obtuse, she raised her mug. 'Taking a break. Want a cup?'

'No, thanks.'

'How's Tipton?'

'Comfortable. I've scheduled him for an angioplasty in the morning.' He waved his arms around the room. 'Is this what you meant by "another plan"?'

Jake's abrupt subject change came as no surprise. 'Yes.'

'So you think that moonlighting is the answer.'

'I need the income. This is the only way to get it. Legally, that is.' She grinned but his face didn't register any humor.

'How many nights do you intend to work?'

'Every other weekend.' Knowing that he'd learn everything anyway, she added, 'I'm also covering three nights a week at a minor emergency center.'

'You're what?'

'I'm covering—' she began patiently.

'I heard that,' he said. 'Do you realize what you're letting yourself in for?'

'It won't be easy, I know, but in order to get a bank loan I have to show that I can pay it back. If I can't they'll turn me down. The only other alternative is to close the Health Center.'

He spoke with caution. 'Would that be so bad?'

'You know I can't.'

'Can't, or won't?'

She fell silent. In the background she heard voices, the

shrill of a distant telephone and the clatter of equipment rolling down the hall. 'How can you ask that? The center is part of who I am. If I give it up what will be left?'

'I don't like to see you run yourself ragged for nothing.'

'For nothing?' Her temper rose. Her hand shook and some of her hot chocolate sloshed over the cup's rim. 'If I worked twenty-four hours a day to build a lucrative medical practice I'd be applauded for my efforts. But if I choose to work several jobs so that I can take care of those in poverty then I'm working for nothing?'

'That's not what I meant. You're setting yourself up for failure.'

'Oh, really?'

He stepped within arm's reach. 'How long do you think you can keep up the pace you've established? How long until you're so tired that you can't see straight? How long until you make a fatal mistake?'

His attack took the wind out of her sails. 'I'm sorry, Jake, but I have to do this. You may not like it, and I can't say that I'm overly thrilled with my schedule, but I need your support.' She turned pleading eyes on him. 'Please?'

He cupped her chin in his hand. 'I want to condone what you're doing,' he said, his voice hoarse, 'but I can't.'

Hurt by his rejection, she tried to break away but his grip tightened. 'I'll stand behind you, but I won't sit on the sidelines and cheer you on. Carrying two extra jobs is a mistake. Once you start you'll never be able to stop the vicious circle.' He dropped his hand.

For a moment she froze, shocked by his vehemence. Unwilling to show her deep disappointment, she hid behind a carefree attitude. 'No one can accuse you of not being honest or outspoken. I certainly know your feelings on the matter.'

'But you're going to proceed anyway. Right?'

A lump came into her throat and she swallowed hard. 'Unless you have another idea?'

The corners of his mouth turned down. 'Not at the moment.'

'Then don't complain about my decision.' She sipped her now-lukewarm chocolate, clutching the mug in a vise-like grip to stop her hands from trembling.

He threw up his hands in exasperation. 'What will it take for you to see reason?'

She stiffened. 'I'll tell you what I see. The Family Health Center doesn't produce a steady income and consequently is facing a financial crisis. According to you, we should close our doors.

'To compensate, I found not one, but *two* lucrative positions to take care of our cash flow problems. Yet you still say we should close our doors.' She set her cup on the coffee-table and crossed her arms over her white lab coat. 'It seems to me that you're not interested in or concerned about my patients.'

'That's not true and you know it.'

She lifted one eyebrow and met the full force of his gaze. It was obvious from his squared jaw, the pulse beating at his temple and his flared nostrils that her comment had angered him. Yet she was furious, too. Even after baring her soul—explaining her motives— he didn't understand. *Wouldn't* understand.

In that moment she knew that her fantasies of a future with Jake were just. . .fantasies.

From outside the room a feminine voice asked in clear tones, 'Anyone seen Dr Holloway?'

The door swung open and Naomi Stewart walked in.

'There you are,' she said cheerfully. 'I've been looking for. . .' As if sensing the tense atmosphere, her smile wavered and her sentence died unfinished.

Jake strode to the exit. 'Talk some sense into her, will you?' With that parting shot, he slammed the door so hard on his way out that the Cupid decoration fell off.

Naomi flicked the tail of her dark braid over one shoulder. 'I don't need to ask how he took your news.'

Kirsten sighed. 'No.'

Naomi walked to the coffee-pot and filled a mug half-full. 'I wonder why he reacted so strongly?'

'He thinks I'm overextending myself.'

Naomi paused, looking thoughtful. 'You are, you know.' She held up her hand to stave off Kirsten's objections. 'Did you ever stop to think he might *want* you to have some free time? For more *personal* reasons?'

Kirsten recalled his kiss and the way he'd fussed over her after she'd been injured. Could Naomi be right? Her face warmed at the thought.

'Do I detect a Cinderella story in the making?'

'More like the Prince and the Pauper.' Kirsten thrust her mug of chocolate into the microwave for a quick reheating. 'He insists that I should close the center.'

'Based on what you've told me, his suggestion is valid. At least from a business standpoint.'

'Yes, but I can't accept it. Do you think I'm crazy to go to this much effort to keep my practice?'

'You're asking me? The doctor who practically lives here at Lakeside in order to stay in the running for a promotion?' Naomi shook her head.

'Yes, I am. And be honest.'

Naomi's expression became thoughtful. 'Even though we both had the same poverty-stricken background, those circumstances shaped our lives in different ways.

You wanted to stay and help others in the same situation while I couldn't wait to put it behind me.

'I feel for those people, but I don't want to live and work in the same environment where we grew up. You had a knack—still do, in fact—for seeing the beauty underneath the squalor and pain while I didn't. So, to answer your question, if you want to pay the price to keep your dream alive then go for it.

'On the other hand,' Naomi continued, 'some dreams aren't meant to be. You have to be wise enough to know which ones are which.'

The vision in which Jake filled an important void in her life fell in the latter category. Her accusation hadn't been totally correct. Jake might be interested in her patients' welfare but, for the two of them to have a future, he needed to be as personally involved as she was. Unfortunately, his caring didn't go far enough. Why else would he always push her to take the easy way out?

Their differences could never be reconciled. They were simply two people whose paths had crossed for a brief time, and her spirit mourned the loss.

Edward's leaving had bothered her but, deep down, she'd expected it and had prepared herself accordingly. Jake, however, had shown his softer side and broken down the wall around her heart. Her emotions were now hopelessly entangled and the only cure was work— something she'd have in large quantities during the coming weeks and months.

Kirsten drew a fortifying breath. 'By the way, thanks for speeding up my paperwork so I could start ER duty this weekend.'

'Since you'd worked here before it was easy.'

'Regardless, I appreciate what you've done.'

'Don't get too thankful, you may regret it after a shift filled with trauma cases.'

Someone pounded on the door and a nurse stuck her head inside. 'Three-car accident is on its way. Eight people involved, including three children. ETA five minutes.'

Naomi drained her mug in one gulp. 'See what I mean?'

'I've reviewed your application and I'd like to ask a few questions, Dr Holloway.' Milton Tate, one of the bank's loan officers, leaned back in his executive chair and steepled his fingers.

Kirsten clenched her hands together in her lap, noticing the fiftyish man's expensive suit, designer silk tie and perfectly styled hair with enough silver at his temples to give him a distinguished air. 'What would you like to know?'

'You've been working at Lakeside Hospital and the Minor Emergency Center for the past two weeks. Are those long-term commitments?'

'More or less.'

He tapped his gold-plated pen on the desktop. 'From what I've seen of your documentation and tax forms, the odds aren't good that the bank will approve your loan.'

The news made her spirits nosedive. 'Oh?'

'The Health Center's financial records haven't been showing a profit.'

'I explained the reason.'

'Yes, well, you may choose to be a charitable institution, but banks have to protect their investment. You understand.'

Of course, she thought. They only lend money to people who don't need it.

'Is there anyone who could possibly co-sign the note?'

Jake came to mind, but she was certain he'd refuse. Her mysterious supporter was her last hope, and she prayed that her written plea would be convincing. 'Not at this time, but I'm working on it.'

Mr Tate closed the file. 'Good,' he said. 'That should sway the committee's decision in your favor.'

He rose and thrust out his hand, which she accepted and shook. 'I'll be in touch, Dr Holloway.'

Nodding her acknowledgement, she strode out of his office and into the bank lobby, where she asked for Kenneth Lawrence—the one man who knew her bene-factor's identity. In less time than she'd imagined she found herself face to face with him, making her request.

Lawrence reminded her of Ebenezer Scrooge and, although he wasn't optimistic, she took heart in the fact that he did promise to pass along her personal letter.

Striding into the parking lot to her car, she was filled with a sense of relief. She'd done everything she could— the final stage of her plan was in motion.

With a tiredness born of overwork, she navigated the thirty-minute drive to her clinic via the Interstate.

Holding the wheel with one hand, she flipped open her black appointment book which was lying on the passenger seat. Her hectic schedule demanded organiz-ation and she was glad she'd trained herself long ago to keep lists. A pharmaceutical sales rep was coming this afternoon, but otherwise she was free. Thank goodness Jake would be at the clinic today to carry most of the load.

Ever since their disagreement several weeks ago she'd expected him to quit before he'd completed his six months. Although the center's precarious status and her extra jobs remained a taboo subject, and although he'd given her a humorous card along with a box of chocolates for Valentine's Day, deep down she prepared for his eventual resignation.

Unfortunately, this Thursday Amy greeted her with bad news. 'Dr Marshall isn't coming.'

In spite of Kirsten bracing herself for the possibility, the news seared her heart.

'He won't be back—'

'Fine,' Kirsten interrupted, covering her pain with anger. Didn't an employer deserve a two-week notice? 'We managed without him before and we can do it again. Let me take off my coat and we'll get to work.'

A few hours later Jake strode into the room Kirsten had provided as his base, facetiously terming it an office. He didn't mind that the area was tiny, cramped and austere: he spent most of his free time in Kirsten's, anyway. Anxious to seek her out, he slung his overcoat over a chair and slipped a fresh lab jacket over his white dress shirt and gray trousers. His briefcase opened with a click and he pulled out several files.

Out of the corner of one eye he saw Amy hesitate in the doorway. 'Sorry I'm so late. Emergency angioplasty.'

'We survived.' The nurse walked in, clutching a chart with both hands. 'Can I talk to you a minute?'

'Sure, go ahead.'

Amy thrust the folder under his nose. 'Dr Holloway ordered an injection of penicillin for an adolescent with strep throat.' She paused to lick her lips.

He waited expectantly.

'Anyway, this patient has a penicillin allergy. I can't give him the shot, but since I'm not a doctor I can't change the order either. He and his mother are waiting.'

'Where's Kirsten?'

'She left a few minutes ago to admit a patient to the hospital. I haven't been able to reach her yet.'

Jake took the chart and, with the stroke of a pen, changed the medication to erythromycin. After scrawling his name, he handed the folder back to Amy. 'There you go.'

'Thanks.'

'No problem. Does, um, this sort of thing happen often?'

Amy shook her head. 'To my knowledge, this is the first incident. She's working too hard, you know. I don't think she's slept in ages—a good night's sleep, that is.'

The news didn't surprise him. The changes in Kirsten seemed more obvious each time he saw her. 'I've already talked to her about it and it didn't do any good.'

'I was afraid of that.'

'I can try again, but—'

'Would you?'

The plea on Amy's face made him agree, although he didn't have much hope of convincing Kirsten to change her work habits.

Suddenly the rapid click of hard-soled shoes reverberated down the hallway and a frantic voice came near. 'Amy?'

Amy peered around the corner. 'Dr Holloway! You're back.'

Kirsten came to a stop on the threshold, her chest heaving with each breath and her face lined with concern. 'Did you give that injection to the Andrews boy?'

Amy shook her head.

Kirsten wilted against the doorframe. 'Thank God. I'd driven about six blocks before I realized what I'd done. I'm surprised I didn't get a speeding ticket.'

Amy motioned to Jake. 'Dr Marshall changed the order.'

Kirsten came to attention, her eyes wide in disbelief. 'Jake?'

'If you'll excuse me,' Amy said to no one in particular, 'I have a teenager to deal with.' She slipped from the room as if glad for the chance to escape.

Jake didn't understand the surprise in Kirsten's voice. 'In the flesh. Speaking of which, your head healed nicely.' The gash above her eyebrow had become a faint pink line. 'Nice work, if I say so myself.'

'Don't change the subject. What are you doing here?' she asked, her arms akimbo.

'It's Thursday. My day, remember?' He shuffled the folders on his desk to hide the name on the outside of one. He wasn't ready to explain why he was studying copies of her sister's hospital chart.

'But I understood that you weren't coming any more.'

'Beg your pardon?'

Kirsten repeated herself. He shook his head. 'I told Amy that I had a tough case and probably wouldn't make it in *today*. As it turned out, I did.' Sudden realization added a trace of acid to his voice—he knew why she'd acted so coolly on the phone. 'You expected to be left in the lurch, didn't you? I didn't realize you thought so highly of me.'

'Don't most people desert a sinking ship?'

'This may or may not be a sinking ship, but you're not the only stubborn doctor in this room. I take my commitments as seriously as you do.'

Her shoulders dropped. 'I apologize.' She turned to leave, then stopped. Speaking to the wall, she said, 'Thanks for taking care of the prescription. When I think of what might have happened. . .'

'It could have been disastrous, but luckily Amy caught it in time. You're lucky she's so conscientious.'

'I know.'

Jake moved behind her and began to massage her shoulders. 'You're tense.'

'Really? I wouldn't have guessed.'

'Crabby, aren't we? When was the last time you slept? I mean a full eight hours, not a catnap.'

She finger-combed the hair out of her eyes. 'Let's see, if today's Thursday then it must have been Monday, maybe Tuesday. I don't know for sure.'

Jake continued to knead the muscles in her back, enjoying the feel of her soft skin and small bone structure underneath his hands. The apple fragrance of her shampoo drifted upwards.

'Mmm.'

Her throaty reply sent his blood surging. He fidgeted, glad that she couldn't see his response. 'If you're this exhausted after two weeks how long do you think you can function?'

She stiffened. Turning to face him, she said, 'For as long as I have to.'

He chose his words with care. 'What if Amy doesn't catch your next mistake?' Without waiting for her reply, he pressed on. 'There's no sin in admitting defeat. You're only one person—you can't carry the entire load by yourself.'

'But these people don't have anyone else.' Her face reflected her weariness.

'Excuse me? The Yellow Pages are full of doctors; it's vain to think you're the only one who's interested in their plight.'

'Then why aren't more of them——?'

'Look,' he interrupted, 'this is a subject we'll never

agree on so let's leave it at that. In the meantime, I'll finish up here. Admit your patient, then go home.'

Expecting an argument, he was pleased that she simply nodded. At the same time, the dejected slump to her frame tore at his gut. Part of him wanted to encourage her—to say that it had been a mistake that anyone could have made—but he didn't. All medical students had the consequences of drug allergies drilled into them early and often in their training. If this episode made Kirsten rethink her position then it was worth his silence.

If only he could make her understand that he wasn't rejecting her patients. He was concerned about the Chester Olsens and Hilda Grants, but he cared more about Kirsten.

No, he amended, he loved her.

For that reason, he knew he had to confront his friend, Sam Bailey. In grim silence he drove toward Sam's house, with Darcy's chart on the seat next to him.

'What brings you out on this cold night?' the sixty-year-old surgeon asked once they were seated in his luxurious living-room. It was funny how Jake had never noticed the opulence on his previous visits.

'I thought I'd ask if you'd be willing to help support the Family Health Center,' Jake said, stretching his arm along the length of the plush white sofa's back. 'Most of the people who go there are in dire financial straits.'

Sam guffawed, folding his smooth hands over his trim middle. 'Give me a break. They'd have money if they didn't waste it on frivolous things.'

Thinking of Chester, Jake struggled to rein in his temper. 'Like what? Food?'

Sam didn't rise to Jake's sarcasm. 'I give my share through my taxes and, believe me, I pay plenty. Besides, I've donated my services over the years.'

Jake seized the opening. 'Do you remember a case about twenty years ago—a little girl, nine years old, with a hot appendix? Darcy Holloway?'

Sam shook his gray head. 'Doesn't ring a bell.'

Jake tossed the folder onto Sam's lap. 'Will this refresh your memory?'

The older man opened the folder and thumbed through the pages. 'I vaguely remember this one.'

'The surgical resident recommended surgery.'

Sam closed the file. 'I didn't think it was necessary. She didn't present with the classic symptoms so I gambled that her condition was something else, and lost.'

Jake couldn't believe the man's callous attitude. No wonder Kirsten had little use for wealthy physicians like Sam Bailey.

'Didn't it bother you that you'd made a mistake?'

Sam bristled. 'Listen here. I was cleared of any wrong-doing. Surgeons are always accused of being knife-happy and yet when we adopt a wait-and-see attitude it isn't good enough.

'I'm sorry the kid died, but she came from a big family—she was a charity case. I probably did the parents a favor. One less mouth to feed.'

Jake saw red. He jumped off the sofa, and in two long steps had hauled Sam to his feet. 'I never realized it before, but you don't have a heart,' he said through gritted teeth. 'And just so you'll know—that child didn't come from a large family. She had two parents who adored her and an older sister who has since gone on to medical school.

'Kirsten is the physician in charge of the Family Health Center that you scorn. She may not have much, but she's a lot richer than you'll ever be.'

Jake released his hold and Sam dropped onto his chair

like a load of bricks. 'You're a disgrace to the profession,' he said. 'Don't get up. I'll find my own way out.'

Leaving Sam in stunned silence, Jake strode outside—slamming the door behind him. The frigid air cooled his overheated skin as he stomped to his car and roared out of the driveway, leaving tire tracks on the pavement.

Now, more than ever, he knew that he had to do something to save Kirsten's clinic. But what? He didn't want her killing herself with work and he certainly didn't want her leaving town. There had to be some strategy that he'd overlooked.

The question nagged at him with the same constancy that a grain of sand irritated an oyster. If only it were spring. . . A few holes of golf always helped him put things in perspective. Unfortunately, the twelve-degree temperature with a wind chill factor of minus ten and the thin layer of week-old snow covering the ground were major deterrents.

The indoor practice range at the golf club would have to suffice, he decided. The ambience wouldn't be the same as the great outdoors, but it was better than nothing. Besides, he could use the exercise.

After two hours of sweating from the exertion of hitting buckets of balls into a net, he had roughed out his plan. By the time he'd showered he knew that it could work.

Now all he had to do was make it happen.

Seated in front of a roaring fire inside Ian Marshall's study, Jake wondered on how many occasions he'd sat in this same chair and used his grandfather as a sounding board. 'I need your help, Gramps.'

A snowy-haired Ian pulled his empty pipe from his

mouth and waved it in the air. 'My son once told me the same thing in the very same way. "Papa," he said, "I need your help." Of course, then it meant he was about to become a father without benefit of matrimony.' His voice lost its far-away quality and he lapsed into the thick Scottish brogue he'd toned down over the years. 'Roy told me you've been seein' Dr Holloway. Are ye tellin' me ye've gotten the wee lass in the family way?'

The comment had been so unexpected that Jake dropped his mouth in surprise. He'd never dreamed that his statement would be considered in that vein although, now that the subject had come to light, he liked the idea of Kirsten having his son or daughter.

Unbidden, he imagined her entangled in his silk sheets, wearing only her sexy smile and peering at him through passion-filled eyes. His body responded to his racy thoughts and he shifted in his seat. 'Sorry, Gramps.'

Ian rubbed his thinning mustache. 'Ach, I should have known. My grandson, the talented heart doctor, is too smart to let that happen. Too bad,' he mumbled. 'Every man needs a family, no matter how much he says he doesn't.'

Jake had always ignored the senior Marshall's familiar lament before. Although he now agreed with his grand-father's statement, this wasn't the time to discuss the family he'd like to have with Kirsten. He steered the conversation back on target. 'I should have said "approval" instead of "help".'

Ian thumped his empty pipe against the free-standing ashtray with an age-spotted hand—the same tray with trapdoors that whisked the ashes out of sight and had fascinated a five-year-old Jake in the process.

'I suppose it's over a lawsuit. Damn lawyers always interfering—'

Matilda bustled in with a tray of cookies shaped into Valentine hearts and decorated with red frosting, a thick roast beef sandwich just the way Jake liked it and two steaming cups of hot apple cider. 'Watch your language, Ian.'

Jake grinned, remembering how her scolding had been meant to protect his and his brother's young ears. Now, however, his grandmother's tone lacked emphasis, suggesting that she did it out of habit rather than true indignation.

She slid the tray onto the small table between the two men and moved to the straight-backed chair on Jake's right.

'Kirsten's been given an eviction notice,' Jake said, 'and can't find anyplace to go. She's working two jobs so she can get a loan, but even if the bank approves her request she'll run herself down trying to make the payments.'

Ian chewed on his pipe. 'And this bothers you?'

'Yes, it does. The pace is too much for her. She's already making mistakes.'

'Why should you care?'

Jake paused to stare into the flames. How could he explain that he'd broken the cardinal rule—don't get involved in the patients? He'd learned a lot from Kirsten, and had fallen in love at the same time.

'I believe in her,' he said quietly. 'And in her work.'

Jake caught his grandparents staring at each other, wearing pleased expressions. 'You knew this would happen, didn't you?'

Ian shrugged one bony shoulder. 'Over the years I'd wanted you to take an active interest in Frank Morrison's work, but you had your own plans. When Steve gambled away the trust fund and you assumed responsibility it was more than I'd ever hoped for.'

'You see, Jakob,' Matilda broke in, 'we've known the center was in trouble but we didn't know what to do. The help we could give didn't seem to be enough.'

Jake nodded. Kirsten had basically said the same thing before she'd embarked on her moonlighting career.

'If there was a way to get the Family Health Center on a solid footing,' Ian added, 'we were confident that you would find it. Kirsten Holloway has a heart of gold, but she has more compassion than business sense.'

'There *is* something we can do, but you may not like it,' Jake warned. He went on to outline his plan, finishing with, 'A lot of pieces have to fall into place, but I'm confident they will.'

A knowing smile crossed Ian's face. 'Do whatever you think best.' He rose and stretched his tall, slender frame. 'By the way, Father Jeffers told me that he's missed seeing you at the last two board meetings. Wasn't one scheduled for this evening?'

Jake groaned. He'd taken over his grandfather's seat on the Catholic Charities board several years ago, and until he'd begun his stint at Kirsten's center last month he'd never missed a session. He weighed his absence against the delay in pursuing his plan to save Kirsten's center.

Suddenly another idea sparked into life. Maybe he'd attend tonight's session after all.

CHAPTER TEN

'I'M SORRY, Dr Holloway,' Milton Tate announced over the telephone a week later, 'without someone to share the risks in case you can't make the payments we couldn't approve your loan.'

Kirsten clutched the receiver with a white-knuckled grip. This was not the news she wanted to hear after spending an entire night at the minor emergency center, dealing with a flood of ill people. Although she'd mentally prepared herself for such an event she'd still kept her fingers crossed.

Tate, however, had wiped away her dream as easily as if it were chalk marks on a blackboard. With the brush stroke of a pen and one red rubber-stamped 'Rejected', she had lost the opportunity to purchase Weller's building.

'If we can ever be of any assistance, or if circumstances should change, please notify us. We'll be happy to serve you in any way we can.'

Hah, she thought, replacing the telephone none too gently as tears burned the back of her throat.

She stared through the window into the parking lot. Even if Weller rented the building to her she didn't have the funds to renovate it. Granted, she could save up the money, do a portion at a time, but that would take years. Unfortunately, without extensive remodeling she couldn't use Weller's property.

A camper parked in her line of vision. Maybe she could outfit something similar—be a doctor's office on wheels, rolling from patient to patient.

Kirsten immediately discounted the notion as too costly. No, she had only one option left, and it gave her a bad taste in her mouth.

She would talk to Carlton—grovel if need be—and beg him to reconsider his decision. Considering that she had less than a month to vacate the premises, she had to visit with the landlord as soon as possible.

Idly she picked up a lab report, noticing that it concerned a patient of Jake's. She laid it aside, then decided to deliver it herself since she was too overwrought to concentrate on her own paperwork.

She dropped the sheet into Jake's 'In' basket on the edge of his desk and pivoted to leave his office. The toe of her shoe caught in a loose tile and she pitched forward. Reaching out to catch herself, she knocked Jake's briefcase onto the floor, scattering papers everywhere.

Oh, for heaven's sake, she thought crossly, crouching to gather the pages together. As she did so her gaze landed on a letter—one that she recognized not only because it bore the Health Center's return address but because she'd written it.

She picked it up, then straightened. Why did Jake have the letter she'd given to Mr Lawrence? The answer came to her and her breath caught. *He* was the nameless benefactor.

'I have to repay a favor.' Jake's words echoed as plainly as if he'd spoken them now rather than weeks ago.

The document burned in her hand. To think that she'd pinned her hopes on a not-so-veritable stranger. How Jake must have laughed when he'd read her request. His helpfulness came with limits, set just high enough to appease his conscience.

If only she'd held firm, refusing to believe that Jake was different from Edward Cox, from Harold Gordon, from Sam Bailey. Instead, she'd succumbed to Jake's practiced charm and quick explanations. She should have known better than to trust or fall in love with someone out of her league.

She tucked the evidence into her coat pocket and stomped into the hallway, intent on finding Jake. Amy, however, intercepted her.

'We're getting stacked up out here—the waiting area is bursting at the seams. Dr Marshall asked if you could give him a hand.'

'You bet I will,' she said grimly. The sooner the patients were taken care of the sooner she could fire the lout. Again. And this time, nothing—*absolutely nothing*—would change her mind.

Amy handed her four folders, her expression tentative. 'Is something wrong?'

'Not for long.'

Although Amy appeared skeptical, she didn't press the issue. 'I've put a mother and her three kids together in the same room since we're running out of space.'

'What's the problem?'

'Flu-like symptoms.'

Kirsten took a calming breath before she walked inside to meet the family. 'So the entire clan is sick today.'

'Afraid so, Dr Holloway.' Mrs Torres, a slender woman of Spanish descent in her mid-thirties, appeared wan and haggard.

Kirsten reviewed Amy's notes. 'Nausea and vomiting?'

'We can't keep anything down,' Mrs Torres said. 'Everyone complains of headaches and dizziness. I also have trouble concentrating.'

'There is a lot of influenza going around. Let's have a quick check and see what's happening.'

She began with the smallest Torres, seven-year-old Jamie. 'May I look in your ears? It won't hurt.'

Jamie turned his dark head without argument, his black eyes dull and his shoulders slumped with weariness.

Kirsten checked his throat, felt his glands and listened to his heart and lungs. Finished with him, she moved to his sisters, twelve-year-old Maria and fourteen-year-old Agnes, both carbon copies of their dark-haired mother.

Once her examinations were complete she was dismayed that she'd found nothing remarkable. Unable to dispel a niggling worry, she asked, 'Does anyone in your family have asthma?'

Mrs Torres shook her head.

Relieved, Kirsten forced aside her apprehension. Fatigue was making her overreact. 'All of you sound as if your breathing is a little forced. Jamie's is the worst, although it could be due to congestion. Have you been missing work or school?'

A sheepish look crossed Mrs Torres's face. 'No. The sickness has gone on for so long now that I can't afford to lose any more pay and the children would never catch up with their classes.'

'You won't recover if you don't go home and stay in bed. If you aren't better in a few days. . .' Kirsten glanced at the calendar '. . .say by Friday, come back. If any of you start wheezing or have trouble breathing then call me right away. In the meantime, drink lots of fluids.'

Kirsten jotted the diagnosis on the last chart. Influenza seemed to be the disease of the week. If she'd written it once in the last twenty-four hours, she'd written it fifty times.

She dropped the chart into the bin to be filed as Amy rushed by with another folder. 'Karen Whipple's having contractions every twenty minutes.'

Kirsten found the expectant mother lying on the exam table with her excited husband holding one hand. 'Is your suitcase packed?'

'It's in the car,' Larry Whipple said.

Kirsten listened to the baby's heartbeat. 'Sounds good. Let's see how you're progressing,' she said, tugging on a pair of latex gloves. A minute later she stripped them off. 'You've dilated to four centimeters. When your contractions are five minutes apart call me, then drive to the hospital.'

Over the next hour, even though Kirsten kept busy, her anger simmered. The instant their last patient, elderly Mrs Rose, navigated her way out of the treatment room with a refill of nitroglycerin tablets Kirsten stopped Jake.

'I'd like a moment of your time. In private.'

His brows knitted in puzzlement at her cool tone, but he nodded and followed her into her office.

'Would you care to explain how you got this?' She withdrew the letter from her pocket and handed it to him.

A flash of pain crossed his features as his gaze flickered over the sheet, then disappeared as he stared into her eyes. 'Spying, or did general nosiness come into play?'

'I laid a report on your desk and accidentally knocked your briefcase onto the floor. I apologize for making the mess,' she said stiffly, 'but I'm not sorry that I learned the truth.'

'I never lied to you.'

'You did, by omission. You *are* our anonymous donor, aren't you?'

'Yes.'

Kirsten leaned against her desk and folded her arms. 'Were you checking on your investment? Making sure we weren't wasting your precious dollars?'

'No,' he exploded. 'My former accountant gambled away the trust fund my great-grandfather established—the same account that earned interest for charities such as yours. Since I'd hired the man and trusted him I felt responsible.'

He heaved a sigh. 'So I followed the original terms of the trust—if it was ever dissolved we were to help the beneficiary with their most critical needs for the next six months. I'd planned to make the contributions as usual, but you wanted another physician instead.'

'So that's why you volunteered to work with me.' She remembered how Jake had seemed so unhappy with the idea and how his offer of assistance had made no sense. Now it did.

'Yes.'

'Why all the secrecy? Why not tell me up front?'

He ran one hand through his hair. 'I suppose I could have walked in and said, "Hi, I'm Jake Marshall, and I can't send money any more because I hired an incompetent accountant." How would you have reacted?'

'I don't know, but you can't deny that you pushed the idea of closing the clinic. Was it so you wouldn't have to waste your precious time or strain your bank balance either?'

Jake's jaw tensed. 'You're being unfair. My suggestion was based on sound business practices. You can't provide something for nothing, at least not for any length of time. Your time was, is, running out.'

'You're certainly doing your part to make sure.'

He looked taken aback. 'What do you mean?'

'My loan was denied—'

'I'm sorry.'

'—for lack of someone willing to co-sign. No doubt it was a *business* decision that made you reject my proposal,' she sneered.

'I didn't reject anything,' he ground out. 'I hadn't given my answer to the bank yet because—'

She raised both hands to forestall him. 'I poured my heart out to you, shared my vision. I thought you saw and understood my views, but you didn't. My patients and their needs don't mean a thing to you.'

Jake's eyes glimmered with fury. 'After the time we've spent together I can't believe you could possibly think that.' He strode closer. 'If I committed a sin of omission then you did the same. Not once did you trust me enough to mention your moonlighting scheme. No, you had to blaze a trail on your own.'

'Because I knew you'd try to talk me out of it.'

'You were right. You have this idea that you're the only one who can solve your patients' problems—that no other physician cares as much as you do. You've set your standards so high that no one—*no one*—can meet them. Then, when everyone falls short, you feel vindicated.'

'That's not true,' she cried, ignoring the ring of truth.

He pressed on. 'If you were honest with yourself you'd see that you can't meet them either. Yes, you're willing to devote your entire life, day and night, to your patients, but what will you have in the end? Diana Morrison did the same thing and look where she is.'

'That's cruel.'

Jake toned down his voice. 'Would your sister want you to work yourself to death? We talked once about having time for enjoying life. You don't realize it, but you've fallen into the same trap you wanted me to escape.'

Amy's knock came tentatively, as if she hated to interrupt but didn't have a choice. 'Karen Whipple called. They're leaving for the hospital.'

Kirsten swept the hair out of her eyes. 'I'm on my way.' She turned back to Jake, her resolve strengthened. 'I've said this before, but this time I mean it. Your favor, your obligation—whatever you want to call it—has ended, Jake. Go back to your fancy practice, your high-tech office building. You don't belong here.'

Charged with emotion, she marched out with her head high.

Over the next few hours her fury diminished but, even so, by the time the Whipples' daughter entered the world the embers still smoldered.

Driving back to the center, she clicked on the radio to silence her riotous thoughts and caught the end of an interview with a fire department spokesman.

'. . .importance of a monitor,' the man said. 'We're convinced of the life-saving value of a smoke detector, but carbon monoxide is a killer. It's odorless so a person can't tell if there are increased levels in his home.'

'What are the symptoms?' the announcer asked.

'Nausea, vomiting, headaches. As the toxicity progresses a person experiences confusion, difficulty in breathing, even fainting. It may lead to coma and death.'

Kirsten froze at the wheel. Now she understood what had troubled her about the Torres family. A cold, clammy feeling descended upon her as she recognized her horrible mistake.

She stepped on the gas pedal and wove in and out of traffic, scanning the streets for a pay telephone. The moment she saw a convenience store she squealed to a stop, blocking two cars in the process. The acrid smell of rubber greeted her as she jumped from her car while she fumbled in her billfold for change.

She dialed a number from memory, counting the rings until Irene answered. 'Look up the Torres family's address,' she ordered without preamble. 'The ones who came in today.'

Apparently recognizing the urgency in Kirsten's voice, Irene recited the information.

'Call 911 and ask for an ambulance,' Kirsten said. 'I suspect there's a gas leak in their home. I'm going there now.' With that, she slammed the phone on its hook. Seconds later she roared out of the parking lot, her tires leaving a black trail on the concrete.

How could she have missed the diagnosis? Was she already too late?

Kirsten arrived at the location in record time. She raced up the sidewalk leading to the Torres' two-story frame house and pounded on the front door. After several tense moments Agnes answered, swaying on her feet.

'Get your coat and go outside. I'll explain later.' She pushed her way past the girl. 'Where's your mother?'

'Upstairs in bed. Same as Maria and Jamie. Just like you told us.'

Agnes opened a closet and Kirsten saw the jackets hanging inside. 'Do you need help?'

Agnes shook her head. 'I can manage.'

Kirsten bounded up the steep staircase. Everything was quiet—too quiet. She peered into the first room and found Maria, who was struggling to rise.

'Can you walk?' Kirsten asked as she steadied the girl.

Maria nodded.

'Then get your coat. Agnes is waiting for you.'

Satisfied that the youngster could make it under her own steam, Kirsten rushed to the next bedroom. Seeing the body huddled under the blankets, she shook it. 'Mrs Torres. Get up. There's a gas leak in your house.'

The woman's eyes fluttered. 'Wh-what?'

Kirsten yanked her upright. Now wasn't the time for politeness. 'I've called an ambulance. You must go downstairs. Help is coming.'

'Ja-Jamie?'

'I'll get him. Now move!'

Finding Jamie asleep in bed, Kirsten gathered the boy in her arms and carried him into the hallway. There she met his mother, inching her way toward the staircase.

'Hold onto my arm,' Kirsten ordered, hoping that she could hold her balance. Struggling under the dead weight of Jamie's sixty-five pounds, she descended the stairs— keeping her gaze focused on each step to avoid tumbling.

The wail of sirens grew louder and she felt a measure of relief. Suddenly the load in her arms lifted and a familiar voice urged, 'I'll take him.'

Looking up, she saw Jake.

'Give him to me,' he commanded.

Kirsten released her burden and followed Jake outside as she supported Mrs Torres.

Paramedics raced around their truck, pulling out tanks of oxygen while the ambulance crews unfolded their gurneys. Jake laid Jamie on one and bent over the boy to assess his condition. 'One hundred per cent oxygen by non-rebreather mask,' he snapped.

Knowing that the special mask was used in these cases because it prevented a person from breathing his own exhaled air, Kirsten handed Mrs Torres to another paramedic who threw a blanket over her shoulders and led her away. Thankful that Jake and the EMS staff had taken over, she remained in the background to watch and lick her wounds.

In spite of her outburst, Jake hadn't deserted her or her clinic—how else could he have known about the Torreses? His presence here wasn't necessary—the EMS team had everything under control—but here he was. What better proof could she have that he *did* care about these people?

A sobering thought hit her—one that she couldn't deny. Jake was right—she *had* condemned everyone who didn't follow her career path with the crime of selfishness and greed. The size of a person's bank account wasn't inversely proportional to the size of one's heart. It was time she stopped using one thing to measure the other. Past time.

Agnes approached, breaking Kirsten's concentration. 'What's happening to us?'

Kirsten motioned to another ambulance attendant. 'I believe your furnace is leaking carbon monoxide. You can't smell it, but when levels of the invisible gas rise in your home you develop symptoms like the flu.'

'Wow.'

'You see, hemoglobin carries carbon monoxide in the bloodstream, the same way it carries oxygen. Unfortunately, when carbon monoxide is present it competes with oxygen for a ride and wins. As it saturates the hemoglobin there are fewer places for oxygen. Without intervention, a person will lapse into a coma and die.'

With her eyes wide and her face drawn with fear, Agnes motioned toward the gurney, carrying her brother. 'Will Jamie. . .?'

Kirsten's throat clogged. She could only hope that she'd been in time. Luckily, a paramedic came to check Agnes and saved Kirsten from having to answer.

The ambulances drove away, with red lights flashing and sirens blaring, while the fire department personnel went through the Torres home with their gas meter. Kirsten sat on the front step, too lost in her thoughts to notice the cold cement underneath her or the nip in the air.

Jake towered above her. 'The boy was the worst, but he's coming around. Lucky thing you called when you did.'

'Yeah. Lucky.' She stared up at his face. 'What made you come?'

'I thought you might need me.' He sat down.

Kirsten gazed into the distance. 'I should have suspected their condition sooner. Their headaches, the flu-like symptoms, Mrs Torres's disorientation and the cold weather all pointed to this diagnosis.'

Jake said nothing, as if sensing her need to unburden her soul.

'At the time I examined them something bothered me, but I didn't dig deeper. I was tired and we were busy. If I hadn't heard the radio interview they could have died. It would have been my fault.'

'Don't be so hard on yourself. I could have been the one to see them.'

She turned her gaze to his. 'But you weren't. I was.'

As two firefighters came out of the house one of them told the other, 'Notify the gas company to check out the furnace and flue. A bird's nest is probably causing the problem.' He stopped next to Kirsten. 'Are you the doctor who notified 911?'

Kirsten rose. 'Yes.'

'Our meter shows high carbon monoxide levels. You made a good call.' He turned to his crew. 'Let's air the place out.'

Jake put his arm around Kirsten's shoulders. 'Come on. I'll buy you a cup of coffee. You're frozen.'

'I'm OK.' She changed the subject, feeling the need to right her wrong before she lost the courage. 'I'm sorry for making those horrible accusations. You didn't deserve them.'

'Apology accepted.' Jake peered down at her. 'Sure you don't want a cup of coffee? Or hot chocolate?'

She shook her head. 'I have some thinking to do.'

He cupped her face with his hands. 'While you're at it, think about this too.' Leaning forward, he kissed her.

She was stunned at first but his kiss soon thawed Kirsten's frozen emotions and became a bittersweet experience, one that she'd never forget. When he broke away Jake helped her to her feet and followed her to her car.

She drove to the health center and wandered aimlessly through the corridors, lost in her thoughts. After exploring every option and trying every idea, she was down to one choice. The only choice.

Drifting into her office, she stared out of the window overlooking the vacant parking lot. The building on the other side looked dark and dreary, a replica of the structure housing her clinic.

A gust of cold wind rattled the windows and she scratched a name in the frost that had formed on the panes. DARCY.

On impulse, Kirsten ambled to the file cabinet and reached for Emmaline. At this moment she needed the encouragement that only a sister could provide, and Emmaline filled the gap of the little girl that Kirsten still missed.

Tears pooled in her eyes, before spilling down her cheeks. 'I'm sorry, Darce,' she said, straightening the clown's ruffles with trembling fingers. 'I thought I could do it but I can't. Not any more.' The wind whipped around the corner of the building, howling a mournful tune as if it, too, felt her distress.

Kirsten brushed at her eyes, dislodging the salty drops on her lashes. 'Jake was right. It took a near-fatal mistake to make me realize that I'm fighting a losing battle. So I'm going to close the center. I wanted you to be the first to know.'

Emmaline's smile didn't waver.

Her hands shook as she replaced the doll in her position of honor. Numb from her decision, she stared at the clown for several minutes.

After a final, heart-rending glance she shut off the lights, locked the doors and walked to her car. The center was hard to give up—relinquishing a dream was never easy—but she'd survive.

Jake, however, was another matter.

His kiss suggested that he, at least, didn't find their differences of opinion insurmountable. Unfortunately, she wouldn't be here to cultivate those mutual feelings. Someday, after she'd re-established herself in a practice at the other end of the state, she hoped to recall these days with fondness rather than with a tremendous sense of loss.

'I'm closing the center,' Kirsten announced early the following Monday.

Amid the shocked choruses of 'What?' from Irene and Amy, Kirsten raised her hands. 'It wasn't an easy decision, but I can't stay on this merry-go-round any longer. You've both been wonderful to work with. I couldn't have asked for a finer, more dedicated staff.'

The sound of someone clearing his throat caught

Kirsten's attention. She turned and saw Jake standing in the doorway to Irene's office, wearing his familiar overcoat.

'Before Irene and Amy look for other jobs I have something to discuss with you,' he said.

It took her a few minutes to find her voice. 'What are you doing here?'

He addressed Irene and Amy. 'Excuse us for a few minutes, please?'

The women bobbed their heads, hopeful expressions on their faces as Jake took hold of Kirsten's elbow and guided her out of the room.

'What's going on?' she asked on the way to her office.

'Are you serious about closing?'

'Do you honestly think I'd joke about this?'

'No, but I just wanted to make sure. I assume you'll be hunting for another job?'

'Goodland and Lakin are anxious for a family practitioner. I haven't made up my mind where I'll go.' It really didn't matter—both towns were beyond commuting distance to Kansas City.

'Would you stay here if you could?'

She walked to the window and stared outside. 'There isn't a place for me,' she said flatly.

'But if there was,' he insisted. 'What then?'

And not leave Jake? Her heart sang. 'Of course I wouldn't leave, but—'

'I wanted to tell you about my idea,' he began. 'In fact, I tried to when you told me about your loan, but I had to make certain the details would come together first. You see, the Catholic Charities of Kansas City is interested in turning an empty school building into a health station. It so happens that it's in this area.'

Kirsten turned. Her eyes widened and hope unfolded like the first petals of a rose.

'They plan to fund it through donations, much like you did, but—and don't take this the wrong way—they're good at soliciting money.'

'That's wonderful!'

'Father Jeffers plans to staff it with volunteers.'

Her excitement dimmed. Working for nothing was fine if one was independently wealthy, but she wasn't.

'However, for continuity and to create a chain of command, he's agreed that a nurse, receptionist and a physician be hired on full-time status.' She gasped and he laughed. 'I see the sparkle's back in your eyes.'

'Sorry,' she said, unrepentant. 'I can't help it.'

'The charity will take care of most of the expenses but, since it will take a while for the project to become financially viable, I've agreed to finance the physician's salary.'

'How?'

'In the past, Roy and some of my colleagues had talked about investing in my family's clinic. I wasn't interested at the time—now I am. Using their capital, I established another trust account. The income generated should cover your salary.'

Her eyes widened. 'You sold your clinic? Why, when it means so much to your family?'

'I still own the controlling interest,' he said. 'As for its importance, it pales in comparison to how I feel about you. I was afraid that if you left, even for the few months it took to get things organized, you wouldn't come back.'

She sank onto the nearest chair. 'When did you decide to do this?'

'I'd always wondered what could be done, but it wasn't until I talked to Sam Bailey that the idea mushroomed.'

'You talked to Dr Bailey?'

Jake nodded. 'After I studied Darcy's medical file I wanted my questions answered. Needless to say,' he said wryly, 'I have one less golf partner.'

She clapped her hands to her face. 'Oh, Jake! I'm so sorry.'

He shrugged, as if the loss was minor. 'Anyway, I also checked with the dean at the med school. Since the health station will be in the same neighborhood, serving the same people as before, it won't affect the repayment terms of your medical school loan. However, if you'd rather leave. . .' His voice died.

Kirsten stood. Crossing the room, she took his hands in hers. 'I don't. You can't imagine how much I want to stay.'

His mouth turned into its familiar lopsided grin. 'I was hoping you'd say that. I didn't like the idea of the woman I love living on the other side of the state.'

Once again his comment rendered her speechless. 'Are you serious?'

Grinning, he nodded. In the next instant his expression turned grave. 'The trust does have one contingency that you should know about.'

Puzzled, she wondered what condition had been attached to make him appear so unsure of himself. She cocked her head and waited expectantly.

'The beneficiary has to marry the trustee.'

Kirsten's jaw dropped. As the significance of his remark penetrated her shocked brain she couldn't contain her excitement. The future no longer seemed bleak, but something to anticipate.

She threw her arms around his neck and hugged him. 'I'd be delighted.'

EPILOGUE

'TODAY's perfect for our open house, isn't it?' Jake snatched an hors d'oeuvre from a passing waiter and popped it into his mouth.

'Yes, it is. Besides, May is a wonderful month for new beginnings,' Kirsten said. With her left hand, she adjusted the medical insignia pinned to the lapel of his navy blue suit. The caduceus wasn't conspicuously crooked, but she didn't want anything to mar her husband's appearance on such an important day of his career.

At the same time, she seized every possible opportunity to touch this handsome man and assure herself that the sparkling gold wedding band which had been on her finger for the past ten days wasn't a figment of her imagination.

Jake threaded her arm through his in a proprietary manner, the sleeve of his dark suit contrasting with her ivory ensemble. 'Nice turnout, too.'

A large crowd milled around them, mostly physicians, their wives and a few civic leaders. Voices murmured approval as each visitor inspected Jake's newly completed clinic.

Jake motioned to a couple a few feet away. 'I'm glad your friend and her husband came.'

Kirsten smiled. Beth had never looked more radiant, except at her own wedding. 'I wish Naomi had felt well enough to share the day with us. We should have waited until fall, you know. Not only will she feel better by then

187

but we could have made our party into an Oktoberfest.'

Jake shook his head. 'After the commotion of construction everyone wanted to celebrate. Our building's face-lift deserved a new name to go with it.'

She glanced through the large plate glass window to the manicured lawn, with its large sign overlooking the street. Mid-America Medical Arts Building. The title, which signified Jake's contribution to her own dream, gave her the same joy and satisfaction as the sign in front of her practice—the Catholic Charities Mercy Center.

'You know,' she said, 'Amanda once told me that if I saw the first star of the night and recited the nursery rhyme from my heart then my wish would come true.'

He bent his head to whisper in her ear. 'And did it?'

Her heart swelled with emotion as she nodded. 'Absolutely.'

Look next month for Naomi's story in
TOO CLOSE FOR COMFORT
as she tangles with Dr Adam Parker
in the final episode of the *Sisters at Heart* trilogy

MISSING LINKS

How would you like to win a year's supply of Mills & Boon®
books? Well you can and they're FREE! Simply complete
the competition below and send it to us by 30th April 1998.
The first five correct entries picked after the closing date
will each win a year's subscription to the Mills & Boon series
of their choice. What could be easier?

1. APPLE	_PIE_	CRUST
2. STRAWBERRY	_JAM_	TARTS
3. MINCED	_PORK_	BALLS
4. PICKLED	_ONION_	RING
5. GRAPE	_FRUIT_	JUICE
6. FRENCH	_BREAD_	SAUCE
7. TOFFEE	_APPLE_	CRUMBLE
8. PEANUT	_BUTTER_	BEANS
9. TANDOORI	_CHICKEN_	CURRY
10. PRAWN	_COCKTAIL_	SAUSAGES

Please turn over for details of how to enter ⇨

HOW TO ENTER

There are ten missing words in our list overleaf. Each of the missing words must link up with the two words on either side to make a type of food.

For example, the word *Pie* links with *Apple* and *Crust* to form *Apple Pie* and *Pie Crust*:

APPLE - PIE - CRUST

As you find each one, write it in the space provided, we've done the first one for you! When you have linked up all the words, don't forget to fill in the coupon below, pop this page in an envelope and post it today—you don't even need a stamp!

Hurry, competition ends 30th April 1998.

Mills & Boon® Missing Links Competition
FREEPOST, Croydon, Surrey, CR9 3WZ

EIRE readers send competition to PO Box 4546, Dublin 24.

Please tick the series you would like to receive
if you are a winner:

Presents™ ❑ Enchanted™ ❑ Medical Romance™ ☑
Historical Romance™ ❑ Temptation® ❑

Are you a Reader Service™ Subscriber?   Yes ☑   No ❑

Mrs/Mrs/Miss/Mr *SUSAN HICKEY*

(BLOCK CAPS PLEASE)

Address *21. THE SCOTCHILL*

KERESLEY

COVENTRY Postcode *CV6 2ER*

(I am over 18 years of age)   C7J

One application per household. Competition open to residents of the UK and Ireland only. You may be mailed with offers from other reputable companies as a result of this application. If you would prefer not to receive such offers, please tick box. ❑

Mills & Boon is a registered trademark of Harlequin Mills & Boon Limited.

mps MAILING PREFERENCE SERVICE

MILLS & BOON®

Medical Romance™

COMING NEXT MONTH

WAIT AND SEE by Sharon Kendrick

Despite getting off to a bad start it wasn't long before Maisy and Matthew were appreciating each others professional and personal qualities! But he had issues to resolve before he could offer her a future with him...

TOO CLOSE FOR COMFORT by Jessica Matthews
Sisters at Heart

Adam can't believe it when he reads Naomi's letter of resignation, *"Please understand my reasons and never forget the wonderful time we had together."* What can he do to make her stay?

SECOND CHANCE by Josie Metcalfe
St Augustine's

When Laura wins a dance with a mysterious stranger at the hospital's Autumn Ball, she can't forget it or his kiss. Wolff was appalled, he'd only done it on the understanding that he wouldn't be recognised—but Laura did...

DOCTOR DELICIOUS by Flora Sinclair

Shy, retiring Beth makes a vow, "To stand up for herself!" She transforms herself and Dominic is shocked into treating her as the sophisticated woman she has become. Who does he really love—the old Beth, or the new?

Get swept away by

RISING
Tides

by award-winning author EMILIE RICHARDS

**The reading of a woman's will threatens
to destroy her family.**

*In this explosive sequel to the critically acclaimed
Iron Lace, family, friends and strangers gather for
the reading of Aurore Gerritsen's will. The threat of
an approaching hurricane becomes a minor incident
as each bequest reveals yet another dark family secret.*

~

Valid only in the UK & Ireland against purchases made in retail outlets
and not in conjunction with any Reader Service or other offer.

50p OFF
COUPON
VALID UNTIL: 31.1.1998

EMILIE RICHARDS' *RISING TIDES*

9 904170 190503

0472 00172